"Adventure in life is good; consistency in coffee even better." ~ Justina Chen, North of Beautiful

PERFECT BREW
BOOK 3

A TRIPLE
SHOT OF
TROUBLE

JO-ANN CARSON

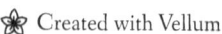

INTRODUCTION

A Triple Shot of Trouble
~ *triple trouble, boil and bubble*~

Can an enchantress stop evil from taking over the world? In the third book in the Perfect Brew trilogy, Cassie Black, a powerful witch with a serious caffeine addiction, faces Erebus, The Lord of Darkness. With the help of a sexy warlock, a vampire who doesn't understand the word "no," and a very-human detective, she searches for a way to banish the dark overlord forever.

It's been months since Erebus raised his head, but when an artist in town is murdered, Cassie knows the beast is back. Using all her resources, she searches for her friend's murderer knowing her efforts will lead to the source of all evil.

Will the body count rise before Cassie catches the killer? Will she vanquish Erebus once and for all? Will her love-life settle down? There's a lot of drama stewing in Cassie's caldron.

A Triple Shot of Trouble is the third and final book in

the critically acclaimed Perfect Brew trilogy. It can be read as a stand-alone or as part of the series. If you like magical cozies with strong characters, romance, and humor, you'll love this novel.

Buy *A Triple Shot of Trouble,* today and enjoy a fun, heart-warming story filled with intrigue, sweet romance, and a touch of magic.

ONE

"Coffee...smells like magic and fairy tales."
Lacie Pinnell, Facebook

"Darkness is coming," whispered Sid. "Doom looms," she muttered. "Evil rises."

Cassie Black ignored her cat's words as she looked out her bedroom window. She didn't need to hear her familiar's premonitions. She felt the truth in her bones. The forces of darkness grew stronger every day.

Cassie lived in the small Pacific Northwest town of Mystic Keep, where magic folk lived comfortably hidden among regular people. With her increasing powers as a sorceress, Cassie found herself in the middle of a supernatural, epic struggle against evil. If she relented her watch, even for a moment, darkness would take over her town, and from there, the world. She groaned. And to think that less than a year ago, she had been a simple witch with so little power she could barely boil water. Cassie studied the landscape in her witch's mind.

A snow owl hooted three times from his perch at the

Lookout. A pack of coyotes standing on the ridge above town lifted their heads to the sky and howled at the rising moon. And in the forest, a cougar stalked its prey with cunning stealth. She was not the only one who sensed what was coming. A palpable feeling of dark anticipation surrounded her, pressing in on her consciousness. Cassie sighed. She hated it when her cat was right.

SANJAY SCOUTED on foot the forested area surrounding the town. His familiar, a peregrine falcon, soared high above him in a midnight-blue sky graced by the light of a full moon. Dressed in black, he carried a demon dagger, warlock sword, and an assortment of magical elixirs. One never knew what they might run into in the woods, he mused. Earlier that evening, he had surveyed the area with his crystal ball, but that hadn't been enough. He wanted to check out every corner of the wilderness with his own eyes. Something was out there watching them.

A chill slithered up his spine. He sensed more than saw the coming danger. How could he, a fearless sorcerer, fall to such an elemental level of panic? He laughed at himself. It was a story as old as time. Sanjay Kahn, the committed bachelor, had fallen in love.

With the coming darkness, he feared not for his own life, but for that of his lover's, Cassie Black. That was the damn thing about love, it made him vulnerable. Seeing her hurt would be worse than being injured himself. With that thought, he picked up his pace and broke into a run to complete the trail through the trees. He wanted to be back in her warm bed, to be with her. He smiled as he watched himself glide through the tall cedars. Falling in love had made him happier than he had ever been in his life. Cassie Black was more than a talented witch. She was his witch.

It was January. The shortened days of light, coupled with cold winter winds slowed the tempo of their small community. Mundanes and supernaturals went about their lives peacefully. Everything on the surface appeared perfectly tranquil.

Perfectly?

If you scratched below the surface, the mirage disappeared. In his warlock's soul, he knew Erebus, the Lord of Darkness, prepared his forces to lay siege on the world. Mystic Keep was his entry point because nine months ago, he had entered their realm through their portal.

Sanjay took his last turn, around a giant fir tree and saw the lights of the town below. Cassie would be waiting for him with open arms.

A flaming message flew towards him. Only The Brotherhood sent him flamers.

His time had come. The warlock elders had summoned him.

TWO

"Today's vibe ...coffee, lots, and lots of coffee.
~Anonymous meme, Facebook

Sanjay's relationship with The Brotherhood hadn't always been fun. Twenty years ago, when a shadow had been cast upon his reputation by a senior member, he had left the organization. At the age of eighteen, he became a rogue warlock, and he had loved everything about his status. The sexy moniker drew lovers better than an elixir of gooseberries and juniper. It also gave him a reputation of note among warriors. Many exciting opportunities for employment came his way, and it seemed he never had a dull moment or an empty pocket. But the best part of being a rogue warlock was the freedom it gave him to be himself, to do what he wanted to do, when he wanted to do it. To answer to no one but himself.

The message in his hand continued to burn. He should open it.

To save Cassie and the world, he went to The Brotherhood and requested to be accepted once again. Knowing he needed their support for the battle that lay ahead, he had offered his allegiance and lost his freedom. He closed his eyes and, and with a simple chant, transported himself to his home.

He stood by the window in his turret. The forces of power closed in on him. In his hand, he held the invitation to his Initiation Ceremony with the Brotherhood. If he took this step, it would be irreversible, as the auspicious supernatural organization would never give him a third chance. He read the message once and released it into the air, where the flame grew and consumed it.

Peregrine, his falcon, and familiar perched a yard away from him on the back of his favorite chair. "There's still time to change your mind," he said

"Not a chance," said Sanjay. "I willingly give my freedom for her. I would give anything to protect her." And, of course, the others, but he didn't need to say that.

He lifted his arms and created a swirling, silver vortex of pulsating energy, a portal to take him to the hall of the mages. He held out his hand for Peregrine, and together they entered the magical portico. Within seconds they arrived inside the Temple of the Arcana, the sacred sanctuary of the Warlock Brotherhood, where warlocks held official ceremonies. Only the initiated could enter its domain.

"You may regret this, warlock," muttered Peregrine.

The Greek styled temple, made of tall marble pillars, elevated floors, and mirrors, sat upon a cloud between dimensions. It held within its structure a mystery of its own. Created by old magic, it was held together by warlock spells and protected by the enchantments of the greatest sorcerers in the universe. It radiated miraculous power as if it were a dream.

Sanjay took a deep breath. It had been years since he

visited this space, and yet he felt at home within it, as if deep down in his heart, the place had never left him. The sorcery within the temple anchored him now as it had since his birth ceremony. A feeling of belonging rose within him. He swallowed. He thought for a moment that his reaction could be a result of the magic flowing around him freely, giving him a sense of euphoria. But his warlock heart knew the truth. He, Sanjay Kahn, belonged here.

"Welcome, son." Arjan Khan stood before him. "I will enter the inner chamber with you. You need not go alone."

"Father." Sanjay nodded. "I apologize for any embarrassment I may have caused you over the years." He had planned to say more, wanted to say more, but his father put up his hand.

"Son, I could not be prouder of you." He wore the formal warlock attire of a member of the inner circle, black leather pants, and a black dress shirt under a magical cape, which hid weapons, spells, and potions.

Sanjay took his father by surprise by hugging him. The older man smelled of the country estate where Sanjay had grown up. Memories he had blocked for years flooded his being. This was more than coming home to the Brotherhood, it was a reunion with his family, his royal family. He had heard from others that his father had not been well, that he had been hospitalized for a heart attack, so this reunion was timely and deeply, heartfelt. They slapped each other on the back.

As Sanjay took a step away, Arjun raised his hand and turned it, dressing his son in formal attire.

Sanjay laughed. "Sorry, I should have thought of that."

"Sanjay, this initiation won't be easy for you this time."

"I don't understand, father."

"You were a boy when you were first initiated. Your

powers were still forming. Now you are a man and a rogue. Shall we say, rough around the edges? The magic they use will be far stronger."

Sanjay nodded. "I understand."

"I don't think you do, son. It will be so strong, you will not be able to go rogue ever again."

Was that possible? Sanjay hesitated. "I am stronger with the Brotherhood," he said.

His father's face drew long. "Yes, yes, that is true. But you know, son, we would still help you if you remained an outsider. You are my son, born a royal warlock, and your battle with Erebus is for the good of all."

Sanjay nodded. "I would never be as strong a warlock on my own, as I will be as a member of the Brotherhood. I must be one with our federation."

"That is true." His father's dark-brown eyes deepened with love.

"Then let us speak of this no longer," said Sanjay. "I want to belong to the Brotherhood."

A slow smile spread across his father's face. Together they entered the circular chamber. "As long as you under-stand, there is no turning back," he said. He led the way to the door.

A young warlock played the harp on one side of the hall. A choir of wizards chanted magic incantations on the other. The air smelled of old spell: a little musty, but powerful enough to tackle anything in the universe.

In the center of the inner council, the elders sat in a circle. Sanjay had expected crowds of onlookers because that is the way it had been the first time he had been initi-ated, but this day only the elders attended.

As they entered Grimshaw, the head of the council stood. "Greetings, Sanjay Kahn." Grimshaw wore the warlock attire in the color of gray to designate his station. Despite being bald and having a bent spine, he was a formidable warlock of impeccable character, and one Sanjay had always revered.

"Greetings and salutations, Master Grimshaw," Sanjay said. He took a deep bow. "I am deeply honored and grateful for this invitation."

"You may stand, Sanjay Kahn."

Slowly, each of the council members stood. Sanjay bowed to each and called them by name. Thomas Brackenfeld, the man who had cast a shadow on his reputation, no longer stood amongst them.

The council members, many of them over the age of a hundred, sat after the introductions, but one remained standing, Wizard Wizendale. A tall, handsome man, with a mixture of Asian and Polynesian features, he had powers rumored to be the greatest in existence. He commanded the room with his presence. As his hand rose, the chants stopped.

"Enter Sanjay Kahn, rogue warlock. It is time for you to become one of us."

"It's your last chance to run. I will stand by you, whatever you decide," said Peregrine in the warlock's mind. When Sanjay didn't respond, the raptor flew from Sanjay's shoulder to perch on a high ledge in the rafters.

Sanjay took a deep breath and entered the inner circle. As soon as he crossed the threshold, a pentagon lit by candles encircled them.

The elders chanted in unison, a spell as old as the first days of the Brotherhood. Sanjay's consciousness faded as he lost all sense of place and time. A kaleidoscope of bright colors, the melodic sound of angels singing, and the smells of warlock magic danced around him. He felt happy one moment, sad, angry, and all manner of emotions the next. In the end, it felt at peace. The chants grew louder, expanding his mind larger and larger until it burst in an explosion of light, sound, and smells from his memory. His body rose horizontally into the air. Pure magic pulsated through every cell of his body until he felt as if there was nothing left of him. He fell to the ground and looked towards heaven.

One by one, the council members came to him and marked his forehead with The Brotherhood's secret sign. With every initiation, he felt stronger.

How long he lay there, he would never know. It felt like an eternity.

THREE

"I'm taking life one cup at a time." ~ Cassie

Cassie waited all night for Sanjay but to no avail. Ice-cold fear gripped her heart as she pulled back the curtains and looked out her window. A dark force seeped through the portal below their town almost a year ago. Now it lurked somewhere out there, waiting for an opportunity to strike. She hated that being her first thought every morning. She exhaled slowly as she scanned the landscape lit by the rising sun.

Evil never remained dormant for long. This Cassie learned from her years at the witch's academy. It hid, grew more potent, and made devious plans. Erebus, the Lord of Darkness, would rise again. She was sure of that. He visited her in her dreams every night, whispering her name in malicious tones. Not wanting to scare others, she told no one. Releasing the drapes, she shivered. Damn the darkness.

With the help of her friends, Cassie had bested Erebus twice, and in her witch's heart, she knew the third time would come soon. It would be the final test for all of them. Either they would succeed in expelling him, or he would defeat them all, and take over their lives.

Good versus evil—a story as old as time. How did Cassie's simple life as a clumsy witch who dabbled in art become so large and complicated? She never wanted to be in the center of the storm.

Sid leaped onto her right shoulder and curled her black cat tail around Cassie's neck. "We'll kick his thorny ass," the cat said.

It wasn't like Cassie to allow herself to be melancholy, but the doldrums of winter seeped into her spirit. Many people suffer from lack of sunlight in the winter, she thought. Maybe she should buy more lights for her apartment.

"You're aching for Sanjay," said Sid. "You two have been hot and heavy, day and night for seven months." The cat wiggled her whiskers. "So. Damn. Hot!"

Cassie frowned. Familiars could be too familiar. Of course, she missed Sanjay. Her warlock lover had disappeared without an explanation, but she wouldn't admit her feelings of longing, even to Sid. At least not out loud.

"Maybe, I need a day at the spa," Cassie said.

Sid chuckled. "A pedicure won't fix what ails you, sweety." The cat wiggled her nose. "Unless a hot guy gives it." Her tail flicked. "wearing a loincloth." Sid cackled. "And carrying toys. Big toys."

Cassie laughed at the thought. "Loincloth?" Sanjay would look good in a .... She shook her head. "You're getting naughty again."

Sid swished her tail. "I'm always naughty."

No argument there. When Sid, whose full name was

Lady Obsidian Black, rescued Cassie from an evil warlock, the cat became infected with a drop of demon blood. The Black coven searched the world for a cure but found none. There was no way to defeat the monster's blood coursing through Sid without killing her. The demon's plasma affected the familiar in unusual ways, and Cassie had adapted to that.

One of Sid's habits was to talk dirty in Cassie's mind. Very dirty. Orgy dirty. And, of course, at the most inappropriate times. Cassie smiled as she remembered being lectured about proper lady-behavior in the principal's office while Sid pushed images of well-endowed naked men through Cassie's mind.

Cassie walked to the door. "Okay, forget the spa. I need a good cup of coffee."

Sid tilted her head and narrowed her eyes. "Seriously? You've been drinking Oscar's specials for the last hour. We both know you have a bottomless cup because it's a magical brew designed just for you. I'd guess you've had at least a quart of the stuff."

Cassie winced and clenched her jittery hands. Yeah, she had had enough caffeine for the morning. "Okay, Sid, have you got any ideas? How can I calm my nerves?"

"Simple." Sid purred. "You need a good tumble in the sheets. Since Sanjay's not here, find a replacement."

"Sid!" How could her cat say that? No one could replace Sanjay.

"It's just sex," said Sid. "A little tickle here and a little tickle there and a big ..."

"Sid, stop it."

"Why not call Alessandro? He's more than willing to please you. And he's got all the right parts." Sid's whiskers twitched. "Is it even cheating when he's so, you know?

Dead." She swished her tail. "And it wouldn't be the first time for you two."

"Sid, stop with the pictures. I warn you. If you don't stop putting images like that in my head, I'll cross anchovies off my shopping list forever." Alessandro of Amsterdam, the most handsome dead man she knew, had been her lover for the last five years. "I'm with Sanjay now."

"Pff." Said Sid. "I'm suggesting a quickie. Well, that's not true. It's never quick with the skilled Alessandro. It's always just the right amount of time to send you to paradise. But, a one-time deal." She wiggled her whiskers again. "For old time's sake. To take the edge off things." She purred deeply. "You know he can calm your nerves and leave you limp. You know he can."

"I don't want to be limp." At least not with him.

"Yeah, right. Like no woman in this world wants to be made love to so passionately, she can't remember her name, let alone the day of the week. Do you remember how he used to ...." Sid sent an image archived in Cassie's memory, flashing through her mind, rocking her system.

Oh, dear goddess, thought Cassie, whose pulse ticked up, despite her resolve. I've got to get Sid off this line of thinking. "No, Sid. Just no."

"Alessandro won't mind."

"I'm sure he wouldn't." Hex, he'd be happier than a vampire in a blood bath.

"Just phone him then. Talking sex isn't cheating."

"Says the cat with no morals."

Sid groaned. It sounded like a panther in pain.

Cassie tisked three times. "I need to take a good walk around town. That's what I need. Fresh air. I'll talk to people about the weather, and feel grounded."

Sid jumped down to the floor, turned to face her, and

rolled her yellow eyes. "If you're choosing to talk to regular people about cloudy skies rather than have mind-blowing sex with Alessandro, you're crazy. Just saying. Besides which—who are you calling regular?"

Cassie groaned. Sid had a point. There's no such thing as a regular person in Mystic Keep. Ever since her great-aunt Ophelia created the magical coffee shop called The Perfect Brew, the town had become a haven for magic folk. Just about every specie of supernatural-being lived in their village: witches, warlocks, shifters, gargoyles, wizards, elves, and even the odd, roaming vampire. For the most part, everyone got along. The mundane population who had built the town didn't know that people amongst them had magical talents, but rumors were growing.

So, who was a regular person in Mystic Keep? Did she even want to get into that discussion with Sid, a part shifter, part demon, familiar? "What I meant was that I need to talk to someone outside these four walls."

"Humph," said Sid as she strode over to the window and jumped onto the sill to capture some rays.

With a flick of her wrist, Cassie dressed. As a matter of habit, she checked herself out in the mirror. In the old days, that is the days before her wacky inheritance; she would have done something wrong. Her sweater would be inside out, her jeans backward, or her socks mismatched. Worst of all were the times when her bra wires warped and pinched the hex out of her. Dressing mistakes happened less now, as her witch powers were growing at an alarming rate. That fact scared her the most.

Her reflection showed a petite woman with blond hair, cut and styled in a bob that framed her heart-shaped face. She wore an ivory fisherman knit sweater over ripped jeans that hugged her curves. Take that, Sanjay, she thought. Light eye-shadow accentuated her green eyes, and passionate-red lipstick made her lips stand out. Why the hex not?

Cassie, now ready to talk weather, headed out to town.

FOUR

"Please, expresso youself."
~Oscar, the barista

Outside, the sun peaked between pink cotton-candy clouds raced across an azure-blue sky as if chased by the devil himself. The brisk, salty wind stung Cassie's cheeks. It was a beautiful day in the dead of winter.

Cassie picked up her pace and marched along the main street of town, looking for small-talk to knock her out of her funk.

"This is stupid," said Sid, tagging along beside her. "You suck at small-talk."

"That may be so," she replied, "but it's a necessary skill in a small town. Besides, small-talk often turns into big-talk." She said everything telepathically to Sid, so no one watching them would think she had gone mad. She laughed at herself. Sometimes she spent so much time talking in her head to her snarky cat, that she wondered about her sanity.

People passed her and nodded. They said, "Good Morning," warmly. That was one of the first things she noticed about the town. Everyone in Mystic Keep greeted you when you passed them. In the afternoon, they simply said, "Hi."

"Dead men have wonderful stamina," Sid said out of the blue. "Stamina, Cassie."

Ignoring the triple-X image her cat sent, Cassie turned the corner of the block. She noticed a gathering outside the community hall, which held a large auditorium and small kitchen. It was the center of town activities. Plays and the town's Christmas pageant were all held there.

She headed over to see what was going on. A beautifully designed sign on the door read, "Artisans Winter Bazaar."

Excited, Cassie entered. Inside, long tables arranged in four rows had been set up for the event. A stream of people carried large boxes into the space. Some unpacked their containers at their table and arranged artwork.

An artist's gala for her to explore! This was just what she needed.

"No, it's not," said Sid in her head. "You know what you really need." She sent Cassie an image of Alessandro lying naked in his bed. He did nude well.

Ignoring her cat, Cassie wandered through the auditorium and caught sight of her friend Zabrina Zafar tempting fate. She headed straight over to her.

Balancing on the top step of a tall ladder, Zabrina was trying to attach a banner to a wooden frame twenty-feet in the air. Cassie held her breath and said a silent spell to steady her friend's feet. The way Zabrina reached out defied the laws of physics, but that was the way Zabrina rolled.

Cassie put her hands on the ladder to steady it. She still didn't trust her magic a hundred-percent.

Zabrina looked down at her. "Well, look what the wind blew in," she muttered through the nails she clamped between her teeth.

"BE CAREFUL," said Cassie waving back.

The artist hammered a couple nails to hold her banner in place and then teetered her voluptuous body down to the floor.

Cassie heaved a sigh of relief. "I hate heights," she said. "I don't know how you do that."

"It needed to be done," said Zabrina. Her round brown eyes, the color of dark chocolate, shimmered against her soft brown skin. Her hair framed her face with a halo of black curls. Everything about the twenty-five-year-old artist beamed a happy, healthy glow. "It's good to see you, Cassie."

Cassie smiled back. She and Zabrina had clicked from the moment they met, sharing their love of art whenever they got the chance. Creating art gets you high, Cassie thought. Not the paint fumes, necessarily, but the process of making a canvas come to life, making something out of nothing, creating art. There was no feeling like it. "Want help setting up?" she asked her friend.

"I think the banner will hold," Zabrina said. "But I could do with a coffee."

"Ah. Okay. I'll see if I can arrange delivery," Cassie said. "I'll be right back. She wandered to the front area, and when no one was looking, used magic to create a perfect brew for each of them in travel cups.

While Cassie was gone Zabrina, arranged a display of different sized prints, and postcards of her work. A large acrylic painting of her labradoodle sat on an easel at the side.

"Your table looks great," said Cassie when she handed her friend a coffee.

"Thanks for the coffee. I really need it. Zabrina took a long sip of her drink. "So, when are we going to go on that artist retreat we've been talking about. I'd like to see your art here next time."

Just thinking about it gave Cassie goosebumps. It would be so much fun. No worries. No responsibilities. Just paint and creativity. "I could look into lodges on the Gulf Islands," she said.

Zabrina gave her a knowing look. "Can you leave Sanjay for a weekend?"

"I need to," said Cassie. "It's been months since I've done art. It's like I've lost a part of me. I feel kind of empty. I'll tell him I need to do art for therapy."

Zabrina took another long sip. "If I had a Sanjay in my life, I'd find it hard to leave him."

"I thought you met someone."

"That's the thing. I'm always meeting someone, but never *the one*. Ya know."

Cassie narrowed her eyes. "You're holding back. What's his name?"

Zabrina laughed. "How do you always know?"

"You have a tell. The right side of your mouth twitches when you're holding something in."

"Okay. Yeah. Well, maybe."

Zabrina opened her mouth to say more and then closed it. She shook her head. "Nope. It's too early to say anything. I'll put a hex on it. Ya know."

Cassie stifled a laugh. Zabrina had no idea Cassie knew

all about hexes. "I know the feeling. So, tell me this. How long do you think it will be before you can say something?"

"Maybe another week. He's kind of jealous all the time, but I think we can work it out. He ..."

A clicking sound from a microphone drowned out Zabrina's words. Cassie turned to see Stardust, a local blues singer, standing on the stage. "Testing. Testing," she called out.

The woman had a polished, bohemian, chic look. Lean enough to pass as a vegan, she wore tight jeans and a loose baby-blue blouse open enough in the front to reveal a good portion of breasts. Long, blond hair and high cheekbones drew attention to her pouty lips. Clearly, she had put a lot of time into looking like she spent no time on her appearance.

Zabrina's face turned red.

Were the rumors true? Was Zabrina's new man Stardust's old man, or were they sharing him? Hmm. Maybe the three of them had a Mystic shuffle going on. Ugh. Cassie had never been able to see what women saw in Kylo. Sure, he had the sexy, Italian looks of a movie star, but he had the integrity of a gnat and the personality of a frog. Cassie wanted so much more for her friend.

Zabrina's lips trembled.

Cassie pulled a small notepad and pen from her purse and scribbled, "We need a night out," she wrote. "Soon." She handed it to her friend.

Zabrina nodded.

Cassie's phone vibrated, and she checked her messages. Oscar had sent her a text, "Trouble at the Brew."

She texted back, "What kind of trouble?"

"The kind." Eye of Newt, she thought. She mouthed, "I gotta go," to Zabrina, and headed for the door.

Just outside the community hall, Cassie ran into Fred Thomas, the town accountant. With his short-cropped hair, a permanent worry line etched on his brow, and expensive loafers, he looked every bit the number cruncher. "This is no good," he muttered. "No good at all."

"What?" asked Cassie. But he rushed past her and continued down the road without answering. At least she wasn't the only one having a blah-day.

Cassie took a deep breath. Yes, something was brewing in Mystic Keep, and it smelled like trouble. Sid wiggled her nose. "And danger," she added.

Cassie entered The Brew, as the antique cuckoo clock rang twelve times. Oscar stood behind the coffee bar armed with a wrench. That's odd, thought Cassie. Surely, he didn't want her help fixing something mechanical. She sucked at that sort of thing. She walked up to him. "What's up?"

Oscar banged the wrench on the side of the espresso machine, and steam rose in the air. "They're upstairs," he said without looking at her. "I wouldn't leave them alone for long."

"Who's upstairs?" asked Cassie.

"Your warlock and vampire."

"Sanjay and Alessandro!" Good grief.

"A Twofer!" Sid snickered. "Your day is no longer blah."

FIVE

"My rule with coffee is that
I can never have too much."
~ Jane Black

Gavin MacGregor, the mundane cop, sat at his office desk, staring at the email from Interpol displayed on his computer screen. Marlowe, his Golden Retriever, lay on a cushion by the door. "What the hell!" Gavin said as he re-read the note. After a string of cuss words, he said, "I knew Cassie Black was a witch, but I didn't know she was a crooked witch."

Marlowe sat up and yawned.

"She's wanted by Interpol!"

Marlowe tilted his head and looked mournfully into Gavin's eyes.

Someone knocked on the office door. Gavin turned off his screen. "Come in," he said.

Brady Buchanon, his younger cousin, rushed in. He stood six feet tall and had a slim build, thick curly black hair and denim-blue eyes. Most of the guys in his family looked like each other, but Brody was Gavin's closest clone, a younger version of himself. And it wasn't just that they looked alike, they acted alike, though Gavin would never admit it outside his head. Was that the reason why he felt extra-responsible for the kid? Maybe.

"Hey," Gavin said.

Brody smiled. "Can I borrow your truck?"

"Hi, to you too. Why do you need my truck?"

"I'm helping Jane set up her business."

"Jane? As in Jane Black?" Gavin swore under his breath.

"Yeah, you know, Cassie's sister."

Gavin grunted. "You shouldn't hang around the Black sisters. In fact, you should stay the hell away from them." He couldn't tell Brady they were witches, as he was sworn to secrecy, and for that matter, they could turn him into a toad with warts. Nor could he tell him that kissing one of them would bewitch him in ways, no human man could survive, because that was too darn personal. Gavin had to think of some explanation as to why his cousin should steer clear of two of the hottest babes in town. He scratched his head. "Aren't you engaged?"

Brody narrowed his eyes.

Not the look of a happy man in love thought Gavin. He raised his brows.

"Jane and I are friends. I want to help her out. That's all," said Brody.

A man going to the slaughter with no idea of his executioner thought Gavin. "Uh-huh. "Her long red hair and blue eyes have nothing to do with this?"

"You left out her hot body. But no. It's not like that. We're friends. She knows I'm getting married."

Gavin had to tell him something without telling him

something before it was too late. "Did I ever tell you about the time I kissed her sister, Cassie?"

Brady's brows shot to his hairline. "Cassie? You and Cassie?" He walked closer and sat in the chair opposite Gavin. "No, you left that story out."

Gavin was known in his family for telling tales. "It was before she and Sanjay got together."

"Yeah. Yeah." Brady said, slowly trying to hurry his uncle up. "So, the two of you hooked up?"

"Not exactly. It's not a long story."

"Gavin ..."

"Cassie came to town for her great-aunt's funeral. I think I told you how she kept running into my sports car. She bent my fender twice."

"Yeah, I heard that one, and about how she had a gun that fell out of the glove compartment, but you didn't say anything about doing a bench press."

The gun thought Gavin. He had almost forgotten about that. Now, Cassie carrying a weapon made sense. Gavin picked up his pen and thumped it on his desk. Cassie knew Interpol was on her tail.

"Gavin," Brody waved his hand in front of him. "Earth to Gavin."

"Oh, yeah. My story. You see, I noticed Cassie was pretty."

"More like hotter than hell," said Brody. "I'm sure you did notice."

"Yeah." Gavin swallowed. Cassie Black was all that and more. "I took her out for dinner, and when I dropped her back at The Perfect Brew, we were at that moment. You know *that* moment ..."

"You kissed her. Wham, bam, thank you, ma'am."

"Technically, no. I told Cassie I was still grieving badly

for my wife." Gavin swallowed. "Which I was." He closed his eyes, remembering the moment as if it had just happened a second ago. "She took my face in her hands, and she kissed me. It was some kiss."

"Oooh! So, what happened next?"

"That's it. Nothing happened next, kid. We talked about a second date, but before we got around to it, she and Sanjay became an item."

"You lost your chance, Gav. I thought you were a better man than that."

Gavin shook his head. "It wasn't meant to happen." A witch and a cop! Never.

"So, you kissed Cassie. So, what?"

"The thing is, it was one hell of a kiss."

"Uh, Gavin. I've been kissed before. I get it."

No. You so don't get it, kid, thought Gavin. "It was not like any other kiss I've ever had."

Brady laughed and stood up. "Let me get this straight. You're warning me that hot, passionate kissing runs in the Black family, and I should be careful."

"Something like that. Yeah. Besides, you're engaged."

"Can I borrow the truck or not?"

"What time do you need it?"

AFTER BRODY LEFT, Gavin turned his computer screen back on. Reading the Interpol alert a second time made him wince. They were looking for a woman who went by the name Black Dagger, who fit Cassie's description right down to her small witchy feet. That's why he had emailed them requesting more information. Black Dagger was wanted all over Europe for art forgery. Before coming to Mystic Keep,

Cassie had been an artist in Amsterdam living the high life, or so she said.

Too many details lined up. But what could he do about it? Cassie and her magic kept the town safe, from forces far beyond his human control. Besides, she was a friend, a trusted friend.

Cops don't have crooked friends, he thought. At least that's what he used to believe. Gavin recalled how Cassie had risked her life for him and the town. Maybe everything in the world wasn't right or wrong. He groaned. Ever since she kissed him, his moral compass had been spinning out of control. Nothing in life was simple anymore.

Come to think of it, before she came to town, his life had been a lot easier. Ignorance was bliss. He had had no idea that supernatural creatures lurked out there. Now he knew, his job had changed. He wanted to protect the town, but he knew he couldn't do it alone. He needed the help of mages.

The sound of Marlowe licking his privates broke his concentration. He laughed. His dog always knew how to make things real.

Gavin composed his email to Interpol:

"Thank you for your timely response. As it turns out, we have no one in the area who fits the Black Dagger's description. Regards, blah blah blah.

It was time to visit Cassie.

SIX

"Without my morning coffee, I'm just like a dried-up piece
of goat."
~J.S. Bach

Sanjay looked out Cassie's apartment window at the
downtown core of Mystic Keep. The cold January day had
ended with a beautiful red sunset over the mountains. It
was, he thought, the perfect evening to return. Perfect,
except that Cassie wasn't home.

Peregrine perched in a tall fir tree across the street,
standing guard. The wards placed on The Perfect Brew
stood more potent than ever before. The portal was safe.
Cassie was safe. The town was safe. It was time to relax.

His initiation to the Brotherhood had taken a lot out of
him, and he didn't want to think about magic, portals, or
Erebus for at least a few hours, or maybe days. He smiled to
himself.

Minutes after he arrived, the air in the room cooled.
Sanjay swore. No one should be able to enter this domain

without invitation. No one. He strengthened his personal protection spells and raised his hands, ready for battle.

Alessandro, the vampire from Amsterdam, materialized in front of Sanjay. "Warlock," he said in his deadly, dark tone.

"Bloodsucker," Sanjay replied. He kept his hands at the ready to take on the seven feet of dead meat if need be. It would upset Cassie, but he could deal with that.

"I found another fissure in your wards, and let myself in," said the vampire in a bored tone.

"I see that," Sanjay said. This could be his one opportunity. They were alone. He could blast the bloodsucker to another dimension, and Cassie would never be the wiser.

Magic always left tells," warned Peregrine watching from afar. "Sooner or later, Cassie would find out the truth, and she would never forgive you. Cassie lived with this dead man for five years, and whether you like it or not, she still had feelings for him."

Sanjay groaned.

"You can put your arms down. I mean you no harm." Alessandro yawned. "This time, the break-in your guard system was created by your re-entry into this dimension. I had been watching and waiting for just such an opportunity."

Sanjay exhaled slowly. He should have predicted that. "What do you want?"

"Cassie." As a slow smile spread across Alessandro's face, his fangs emerged, and he hissed.

"We've already had that discussion."

"Yes. Yes. We will let the lady choose. But..." Alessandro stared down at Sanjay.

"What?"

"You promised to protect her. That was the deal."

"I do protect her with my life, my heart, and my powers."

"You left for over twenty-four hours, warlock. What if something had happened? What if Erebus had attacked?"

How the hell did the predator know about his absence? "I don't have to answer to you," Sanjay said. "But if you must know, I was called away unexpectantly. Warlock business." He exhaled noisily. "You should know, Cassie is protected at all times, whether I'm here or not. While I was gone, my friend, Donovan O'Reilly, the leader of the Warriors, watched over her. Oscar stayed in the guest unit downstairs. Her sister Jane, who, as you know, is a formidable witch, slept in the guest room. Cassie is never alone."

"I understand the Warlock Brotherhood summoned you." Alessandro walked around Sanjay, looking him over carefully as if he was inspected a slab of meat.

"No comment," Sanjay said. "Warlocks never discuss Brotherhood business with outsiders."

"My spies tell me you are one of *them* again." Alessandro looked him up and down and licked his lips. "You are still a rogue at heart, but have become stronger." He sniffed him near his neck. "I imagine your power must have doubled."

A hundred-fold, night stalker, but I'm not telling you that. Sanjay shrugged and looked away.

Alessandro's nostrils flared. "All that magic looks good on you, warlock." He now stood close enough for Sanjay to smell the vampire's northern ancestry, manly sweat, and the blood of his last victim, a willing girl.

"Are you hitting on me?" Sanjay asked.

Alessandro drew nearer still. "You wish."

SEVEN

"Better latte than never."
~ Anonymous

The light in the room shimmered as Cassie materialized between them. She took one look at each of their faces and crossed her arms. Double trouble, she thought. There was enough testosterone in the room to sink a battleship.

Alessandro spoke first. "He left you, Cassie. You of all witches should know, you can never trust a warlock."

"I had my reasons," said Sanjay,

"I don't care about your reasons. Cassie could have been killed while you were away." Alessandro said.

They both looked at Cassie for a response, but before she could manage one, Gavin McGregor strode into the room.

"The cop," said Alessandro.

Cassie sighed. Maybe the presence of a mundane would calm down the anger brewing in the room. "Hi, Gavin."

Gavin checked out the two men and frowned. "You," he said to Alessandro, "have returned."

"That I have," said Alessandro.

The cop looked at Sanjay and Cassie, but they weren't saying anything. "I know all about your kind, now," he said to Alessandro.

"No, Detective. You think you know, but trust me, you do not know about *my* kind."

Gavin squared his shoulders. "I know you're not human."

Alessandro smiled. "Hmm. Did you know that from your human stench I know your blood type is A+, you ate a chicken burrito for lunch and that you haven't had a woman in a very, very long time. That's rather a sad existence, don't you think?"

"What are you?" asked Gavin, still not looking afraid.

"I am Alessandro of Amsterdam, a vampire you should fear. Cassie lived with me for the last five years, and I want her back. I am here to protect her." He nailed the detective with his vampire glare: part charisma, part terror. "Is that clear enough for you?"

Sanjay stared at the bloodsucker. "I belong to Cassie," he said.

Sid purred.

"It's as simple as that. I belong to Cassie. If she decides she wants a different man, then so be it. But I won't let anyone force themselves on her." He conjured a wooden stake into his hand. "Or turn her."

Alessandro shrugged. "I am a patient man." He winked at Cassie. "You know this about me, my love. I can be very, very patient."

Cassie winced. An angry pit of fire burned in her belly. Did any of them care about her, or was she just an item to fight over? And, when the hex would Sid stop purring! "Gavin, why are you here?" she asked.

Gavin blanched. "Oscar said I should walk right in." He cleared his voice. "Did you know Interpol is looking for you?"

Cassie's chest tightened. "You mean they're looking for someone known as The Black Dagger."

Gavin narrowed his eyes. "Cut the crap, Cassie. The Black Dagger is you, isn't it? That explains why you had a gun in your car when I met you, why you are always uneasy around me, why you don't tell me everything I want to know. Why ..." He trailed off.

She didn't say anything.

"I thought it was because you were a witch. But it was more than that. You are an art forger. A criminal wanted by international police forces."

Alessandro wandered to the window and stared out at the night. Sanjay took a seat in the club chair by the fire, closed his eyes, and leaned back.

Cassie looked at Gavin and sighed. "So, what if I was a criminal in my past life? You wouldn't turn me in."

GAVIN RUBBED HIS CHIN. "No. I would never turn you in." Was it magic? Had she bewitched him so much when she kissed him that he couldn't cross her? No. It was more than that. "You are my friend," he said. "You protect the people in this town. I would never turn you in."

"Good. That's settled then. Is there anything else I can do for you?"

Gavin paused. Why was she trying to get rid of him so quickly? Were they a threesome or something? Is that what supernatural beings do?

"No," said Sanjay from his chair. "We are not a threesome!" Obviously, the warlock could read his mind. What the ...?

Alessandro didn't flinch. He reminded Gavin of a bird dog, the way he stood rigid, ready for action.

Cassie put her hand on Gavin's chest and gently pushed him back towards the door. "I was an art forger. A damn good one. But that's behind me. I won't cause you any art problems."

"For now," mumbled the vampire, who tossed his long mahogany locks. He looked like a guy on a romance cover, a super-sized Don Juan.

Sanjay groaned.

Cassie rolled her eyes. "Gavin, I really need to sort these two out before they fight. Vampires and warlocks never get along, and these two are unbelievable."

Vampires! Gavin cussed. "Okay. I'll leave. I told Interpol that no one fitting the Black Dagger's description has been seen around Mystic Keep. I just wanted you to know that." He noticed Sanjay's grip on the wooden stake tightened. "But they won't stop looking, because they think you're involved with organized crime."

Cassie said. "Yes. I know what they think."

"I came to warn you. That's all." Gavin turned and let himself out. Would the vampire and warlock tear each other apart? Maybe that would be a good thing. It wasn't his circus. But, on second thought, he hoped Sanjay would win because he didn't like the idea of a hungry vampire prowling around his beat.

What the hell had happened to his life—his world? He now considered living with warlocks, a better option than living with vampires. What kind of new-normal was that? He let the front door to the coffee-shop slam behind him.

. . .

CASSIE TURNED to her former lover. "Alessandro, as you can see, I am fine. Thank you for your concern. Please leave."

The vampire chuckled. "I like it when you get bossy. It makes me hard."

Sid purred louder.

Darn that horny cat, thought Cassie. "Please, leave," she said to the vampire.

Alessandro vanished.

Now to deal with Sanjay. Where the hell had he been? Why didn't he contact her? She had so many questions. Cassie walked over to him.

Sanjay snored, but in his hand, he gripped the wooden stake.

Cassie's anger faded as she looked at her lover's face. She angled her hand and chanted a spell, landing him in her bed. That's where he belonged, she thought, as she covered him with a blanket. She changed into her nightgown and climbed in under the covers beside him. No checklists or apps to tend to. No missing man in her life. No worries. For once in a very long time, she looked forward to a peaceful sleep.

But, of course, that was not the case.

EIGHT

"Hocus pocus, I need coffee to focus."
~Anonymous

At one in the morning, the emergency alarm at The Perfect Brew went off, causing the building to shudder. Cassie and Sanjay woke to the lights blinking, the floor undulating as if it were an angry sea, and alarms ringing. The sentient coffee house spluttered. "Danger. Beware. Danger. Imminent threat. Danger. We are in Danger!"

"What the hex?" said Cassie. Sid jumped onto the bed beside her.

Sanjay reached up and caught a flaming message. "It's from O'Reilly."

Cassie sat up. Donovan O'Reilly was a good friend of Sanjay's and the leader of the supernatural police force they created to protect the town.

"There's been a murder," said the warlock. Peregrine flew into the room and perched on his shoulder.

Cassie used magic to dress and ran to the window. The

full moon shone over the landscape. The town looked perfectly calm. "Did Donovan say who was murdered."

Sanjay came up behind her and put his arms around her waist. "It's not good news."

Cassie swallowed. "Just tell me."

"It's Zabrina."

Noooo! Grief speared her heart, but she didn't have time to fall apart. Too many lives depended on her.

"Take me there now." Of course, she could have gone on her own, but Sanjay's magic was faster than hers.

"As you wish." Sanjay created a swirling vortex of energy, and they stepped through it to arrive at the scene of the crime.

The loft Zabrina lived in had been part of a warehouse where they made netting for fish boats in the early 1900s. Built beside the docks, the red-brick building had large windows that overlooked the harbor. Ten years ago, the abandoned building had been converted into five lofts, not fancy ones like in the city, but functional ones with a fantastic view. Several artists and one writer lived there now.

Zabrina's loft was tall and narrow. Her art studio took up the main floor. Two wooden easels stood in the middle of the space with partly finished paintings on them. The original wooden plank floor, anchoring the room with its storied past. A stack of pictures of different sizes leaned on one wall, and a smaller pile of blank canvases on the other. One corner of the room had a desk and shelving unit that held all her art supplies, another had a sink and espresso maker. Everything had a place in Zabrina's studio, and everything was in its place, in a creative way.

A spiral wooden staircase led to an open second floor,

which contained Zabrina's bedroom, a small sitting area, and a kitchen. Looking up, Cassie's breath caught for a moment. That must be where Zabrina lay.

"Upstairs," called Donovan from the second floor.

Cassie didn't breathe until she reached the top.

Zabrina lay on her back on a Queen-sized bed covered with a pristine-white duvet now stained with blood. She wore a long, black tee-shirt.

"Zabrina," she whispered as she reached her body. A knife protruded from her friend's chest, and blood flowed from the wound. "Zabrina."

Sanjay put his arm around her shoulders. Sid leaned into her legs.

Donovan O'Reilly cleared his throat. He stood by the window, looking out at the sea. A tall and exceptionally fit man with a good understanding of magic and warfare, Cassie considered him to be the perfect leader for their supernatural, police force. A mature warlock and trusted friend, he cared deeply about the safety of their supernatural world. Thick, unruly black hair fell over the collar of his jean jacket. "Her body's still warm," he said.

"How did you know it happened?" asked Sanjay.

"Angelina, one of our most talented telepaths, felt Zabrina scream. She notified me immediately. We pieced together the location, from the sensory details she experienced."

Cassie scanned the room with all her senses.

Donavan sniffed the window casement. "Hmm." He lifted his left hand and turned it. A yellow mist flowed from his fingertips and swirled around the window. With a snap of his fingers, the fog returned to his heart chakra. He closed his eyes for a moment. "Hmm." He lifted his right hand, whispered a message, and flicked it into the air as a flaming message.

Donovan turned towards them and folded his arms. "I'm sorry, Cassie. I know Zabrina was a friend of yours. You have my deepest condolences."

"Yes," said Cassie. "Thank you." She wanted to hold Zabrina in her arms, but she didn't want to contaminate the crime scene. "I just saw her today. And she looked so happy. And we had plans to get together. And ..." She stopped herself from rambling. But in her head, she kept on. They had so many plans. Now, they would never have a painting retreat. Her eyes welled with tears, and her body trembled.

O'Reilly kept his eyes on Sanjay. "Our shifters were here. They've left to follow the murderer's scent. Cassie should phone her friend in the police force."

"Gavin. Yes, of course," Cassie said as she swiped at a tear rolled down her cheek.

"I smell anger and sage and ..." Sanjay's voice trailed off as he sniffed the air.

"Exactly," said Donovan. "There's another smell, I can't identify either."

"And the wound?" asked Sanjay.

"It's a street knife. There's nothing special about it. No magic. One thrust, straight to the heart. It would appear we are hunting a mundane with a good aim."

"Will you put the rest of the Warriors on the case?" asked Cassie.

The warlock captain flinched at her request. His Irish blue eyes brightened with magic, and he nodded. "I'll keep you informed, Cassie." His voice was unusually soft. "Trust me. I will find out who did this." He vanished.

Cassie wandered around the room, soaking in vibrations. "I can feel the anger too. Perhaps an argument. Perhaps, I can recreate the moment. I'll ask Bob."

Sanjay and Sid rolled their eyes in unison. Bob was Cassie's crystal ball, and while useful, he had the maturity of a thirteen-year-old boy who enjoyed burping the alphabet.

"Okay. Okay. I'll call Gavin," said Cassie.

NINE

"I'm not a doughnut cop. I'm a coffee cop, and I like mine strong." ~ Gavin

Gavin arrived ten minutes later, with ruffled hair and just enough scruff covering his square jaw to curl a woman's toes. It was the first thing Cassie noticed because she had never seen scruff on Mr. Clean-Cop. It looked good.

Sid purred.

"I thought I'd come alone, first," he said, as he walked around the room. "In case there were things you wanted to tell me off the record."

Cassie nodded. "That was wise." She scanned the room, checking once again for strange energy. Sensing none, she started her explanation. "A telepath heard Zabrina's death scream and notified the Warriors. Donovan O'Reilly contacted us twenty minutes ago. Donovan sent shifters out to track the murderer, and Sanjay's gone home to scry the area. I was given the job of talking to you."

"Efficient." Gavin nodded. "Where is her body?"

"Upstairs." Cassie pointed. "On the bed, with a knife ..." Words stuck in her throat.

Gavin put a firm hand on her shoulder. "Cassie, you're in shock. Witch or not, you are in shock. You need to sit down."

"I know. I know. But I don't want to contaminate the scene."

"Honey, you're pale and shivering. I don't care if you're some super-powered supernatural being. Your friend is dead, and your world is spinning. You need to sit down." As he said this, he typed a message on his phone.

Cassie nodded. "I can handle this. Just tell me what you need me to do."

Jane materialized beside her, wearing the unicorn tee-shirt she loved to sleep in. "Cassie." She opened her arms and enveloped her sister in them.

"That," Gavin said. "Just that." He headed up the stairs and called back over his shoulder. "Stay there, Cassie. Don't move around. I'll come back to you."

"JANE, how did you know to come?" asked Cassie.

"Gavin sent me a text. He said you needed me. What happened?"

Cassie told her about Zabrina's murder. They both cried, and their familiars, Sid and Vixen, lay by their feet.

Cassie took a deep breath. "Didn't you hear the alarms at The Brew?"

"No. I didn't hear a thing. I'm guessing The Brew was only talking to you guys. I slept soundly."

"Do we know anything about the murderer?" Jane asked.

"Nothing, yet. Sanjay and the Warriors are on it."

Gavin returned to them. "You're looking better, Cassie." He nodded to Jane. "I called it in. Is there anything more you need to tell me before the examiners arrive?"

"No. I've told you all I know," she said.

Gavin squeezed her shoulder again. "I'll keep you updated on what we find out. You do the same."

"Donovan thinks the murderer is a mundane, but that doesn't rule out the possibility that they were influenced by supernatural forces. I'll let you know if they find anything."

"Okay." Gavin stretched his neck muscles. "Here's our story, ladies. You, Cassie, couldn't sleep and came to see Zabrina for a late-night girl talk. The door was open because she never locks it. You found her dead on her bed and called me at 1:00 a.m."

"Okay. Got it," said Cassie. "What about Jane?"

"You called her right after me."

Cassie nodded. "Do I have to stay and answer questions."

"Uniform officers are on the way to secure the scene. The doc has been called to start the medical investigation. When everyone is swirling around, I'll do a formal interview with you, and I'm hoping to send you home within an hour." He looked at Jane for support. "Jane can stay with you, and if it all gets to be too much, just faint, and I'll send you home sooner."

Cassie folded her arms. "The faster we can get this charade over, the better. I'm good." The lie tasted sour on her tongue. Her shakiness had receded, only to be replaced by a dull numbness.

The sound of sirens in the distance cut through the silence of the night.

"Gavin, can I take Cassie's place?" said Jane.

He looked at her. "In my experience, the closer we

remain to the truth, the better. But I appreciate your support in this, Jane."

Jane smiled at him. "Hey, I'm not just a pretty face," she said.

"I know that," he said, and looked away. "You're another witch." He ran a hand through his messy hair, which normally stayed in place with gel.

"Here," said Jane. She waved her hands over his body and quietly spoke a spell. His hair settled into place. His whiskers disappeared, and his clothes looked fresh and ironed.

Gavin looked down at himself and laughed. "I could get used to having witches for friends." He smiled. "Thanks."

The cop Cassie called Extra-hot came in first, with another uniform she didn't know. Extra-hot got his nickname from the female staff at The Brew because he always ordered his coffee extra-hot, and he was extra-hot himself. In a cop with handcuffs kind of way. Gavin gave the two cops orders, and they set to work securing the scene.

More police arrived. Some of them put on white bunny suits. One had a camera, another a sketch pad, and a measuring tape. The doctor who lived outside of town arrived last.

Cassie and Jane stood at the bottom of the stairs. "I feel like I'm in at a ticket turnstile in the middle of a TV cop drama," said Cassie.

"It could be worse," said Jane.

Cassie felt her brows rise. "How's that?"

"You could be the victim."

Despite herself, Cassie laughed.

Gavin came down with Extra-hot on his heels. "Are you two doing okay?'

Before they could answer, Extra-hot reached the

bottom. "Gavin, what gives?" His cop eyes bored into Gavin's. "When you left me at the bar around midnight, you had a serious five-o'clock shadow happening."

Gavin smirked. "And I thought you didn't notice me."

"Cut the crap. There's something fishy about all of this." He looked at the women. "And why is it that whenever anything strange happens, one of these women is involved?"

"Listen, buddy. You're a good cop and an excellent detective, but you're not looking at the right details."

"Gavin, talk to me. I've got your back. I've known you since second grade. I was the best man at your wedding. I set up the best stag party this town has ever seen, and we did some things we shouldn't have. So, talk to me. You can tell me anything."

Gavin took a deep breath. "Yeah, we need to talk."

Cassie glared at him.

"But not now, and not here, buddy. I need you to handle the show upstairs for a few minutes. I need to question Cassie. She was first on the scene." He pulled his official notepad out of his pocket.

Extra-Hot slid his eyes over to Cassie. "Be careful," he muttered to his boss. He turned and walked back up the stairs. Over his shoulder, he muttered. "I don't trust that one."

GAVIN RUBBED HIS TEMPLE. "Alright, ladies, let's talk in the corner. There's more privacy there."

They walked in silence to where Zabrina kept her art supplies. She had them neatly organized by type, color, and texture, a system he had never seen, but he wasn't an artist.

"Cassie, tell me again what happened."

She repeated her earlier story leaving out any mention

of a clairvoyant, shifters, or warlocks. As she spoke, Gavin took notes, but he also watched her face for tells. She appeared to be telling the truth, but then again, she could have put a spell on him. And then there was her sister the hot red-head beside her, trying to look innocent. He sighed.

"Gavin?"

"What?"

"You sighed."

He waved his hand. "I'm just tired. Go on with your story."

Cassie talked on.

Jane's bewitching powers were far more overt than her sister's. Every bit of her looked like an enchantress. Had the little sister put a spell on him? He should have drunk more beer.

Cassie talked on. He looked at his page of notes, and they made sense enough.

"Okay," he said, interrupting her mid-sentence. "I think I got enough. You ladies should head home and try to get some sleep. I can send an officer with you if you want."

Jane's eyes widened.

Gavin cursed to himself. Of course not, he thought. They could blink out of here on their own. "Or not," he said, with an official smile. "I'll get back to you. Don't be leaving town."

CASSIE WISHED she could read Gavin's mind. He was acting so weird. Her oldest sister, Merlina, had that talent. But not her. All she could do was wonder. Or, she could spell him. But this was hardly the place or the time. Even though her magic had much improved, she hesitated. With her luck, he would turn into a frog.

"But then you could kiss him again," said Sid in her head.

"Don't mind, Gavin," said Jane, who put her arm around her. "He's still adjusting to us being witches. Everything will seem more normal in the morning, after coffee."

"Yeah, you're probably right," said Cassie. "Let's walk. I need fresh air and a little moonlight."

The town looked peaceful. But every fiber of Cassie's body knew it was not. Somewhere beneath its quiet façade hid a murderer.

"Tomorrow," said Jane quickening their pace.

"Tomorrow," said Cassie.

TEN

"How do I take my coffee? Preferably in silence." ~
Stardust

Cassie gave up trying to sleep and spent the few hours left before dawn, looking out at the full moon. Surely darkness was not meant to take over her town. Surely that could not be the intent of the universe. Didn't good always triumph? Or did that only happen in fairy tales?

There had to be a way to stop the Dark Lord.

Dawn broke the horizon at seven. Early morning light fractured the thick mist that blanketed the town. Cassie threw on clothes and headed down to the coffee shop, leaving Jane to sleep in.

Her crew of kitchen witches was busy setting up for the day. The smell of coffee and magic mingled in the air. Usually, that smell and the buzz of morning activity brought her spirits up, but not today. It seemed busy, like a routine on speed. She marveled at how the world continued to spin as if nothing had happened as if nothing was happening. But Cassie knew better. She took her usual seat at her favorite table by the fireplace.

Oscar plunked a special brew in front of her. She took a sip. It didn't take the pain away, but it did taste like a tiny slice of heaven. Focus on what you can control, she told herself. Focus. She took another sip.

"Sid, we're going hunting," she said out loud.

Sid sat up straight and wiggled her whiskers. "Do you think that's wise?"

"I don't care if it's wise. I'm going to find the murderer."

"Cassie ..."

"We'll start with Stardust. See what she knows."

STARDUST LIVED with a group of musicians in a run-down house on Moby Dick Lane, one of the backstreets of town. One could say, on the other side of the tracks, though no train ran through town. The salty air had peeled the white paint on the siding, exposing weathered fir. The moss-covered roof shingles grew tiny forests of their own. The storm door hung at an angle resting on one rusty hinge.

Cassie climbed the wooden stairs to the door and knocked.

No answer. She knocked again. Still no answer. She tapped the third time.

"Okay. Okay, already." A voice called from inside. Keep your pants on."

"Shouldn't she say shirt?" said Sid.

Cassie shrugged.

The door opened wide, which was usual in this town because people trusted each other. She hoped it would always be that way.

"What do you want?" the woman said.

"Stardust. You're the person I want to talk to." Cassie walked into the room before the woman could think about it.

"Uh. Okay," Stardust slowly closed the door. "I guess you can come in." She ran a hand through her hair, pushing it away from her glazed, brown eyes. On stage, the woman looked terrific, but without her inch of makeup and special lighting, she looked human, and stoned, or maybe hungover. Hmm. Probably a combination. Cassie guessed her to be about thirty. Her straight blond hair was pulled back into a single braid, revealing a long face with a thin nose. Her mouth looked pouty. It could be botox or a good night in the hay.

"You know it's early, right?" the singer said.

"This can't wait," said Cassie, who did a quick glance around the entranceway and stared at the singer.

Stardust winced. "Cassie, right? From The Perfect Brew."

"How well do you know, Zabrina?" Cassie said.

Stardust rolled her eyes. "Did someone put something in your coffee this morning?"

Cassie considered spelling the woman. "I need to know about you and Zabrina."

"Whoa. There was no me-and-Zabrina." She swore. "Anyone ever tell you, you suck at small talk."

"Every day," murmured Sid in Cassie's head.

A wave of grief flowed through Cassie. It wasn't easy talking about Zabrina. "I'm sorry. It's just." She stopped. "Just tell me if the rumors true. Did she steal your lover?"

Stardust folded her arms. "I want you to leave."

"Kylo Botticelli. Did she steal him from you?"

"Did I hear my name?" said a man descending the stairs.

"Kylo, this is Cassie, the coffee lady. The bitch is leaving."

"No, I'm not."

Stardust attempted the stink eye, but she had no idea that Cassie, having come from a family with five sisters, had weathered much worse stinky-stares in her life. "I have to talk to you two."

Kylo, a devilishly handsome Italian man, wearing nothing but a pair of blue boxer shorts—but wearing them exceptionally well—walked over to stand beside Stardust. They both looked at her as if she had lost her mind. Perhaps she had.

"I'm sorry. I ..." She took a deep breath. "Have the police come yet?"

"Police!" Their eyes bulged, and their fingers twitched. "We've done nothing wrong." The way they looked at each other was far from convincing. Could they look more guilty? Drugs ... probably. But murder?

"They're on the way," Cassie said with some satisfaction, even if it wasn't right.

"Why?" asked Stardust.

"Last night, Zabrina was murdered. I know you two were, uh, close. It won't take the police long to figure that out and come knocking."

Kylo swore. "I'm out of here." He ran up the stairs with the agility of an athlete.

"So, he stayed over last night."

Stardust nodded. Her face turned ashen white.

"All night?"

"He came home with me after I finished my gig at the bar. We've been here ever since."

"What time?"

"About one."

"So, are you two ...?"

"You think the police want to talk to us about Zabrina?"

"Well, the rumor is that Zabrina stole your man. That makes a great motive."

Stardust nodded. "It's not that simple."

"Never is," said Cassie.

"Kylo and I have an open relationship. If he wants to play around, it's okay with me. I like to roam a bit myself. We consider ourselves liberated."

"How does Zabrina fit into this?

"She and Kylo had a short fling, but he said it was dying out. I said as much to Zabrina at the bar the other night, and she lost it. I suggested we have a three-way, and she insisted he was in love with her—only her. The woman was delusional. You know, a real artist type. Anyway, we got into a catfight." She pulled her hair away from her cheek to show off a scratch. "Roger, the bouncer broke it up and threw her out."

"Zabrina was a good friend of mine."

"I'm sorry for your loss. But you had to know Zabrina had bad luck with men."

"So, let me get this straight. Between eleven and midnight, were you singing?"

"At The Rusty Anchor in front of a full audience. Kylo sat in the front. I had eyes on him at all times. I'm telling you, we had nothing to do with her murder."

"Okay, that rules you both out." Unless they had someone else do the deed. "Do you have any idea who would want Zabrina dead?"

"I'd check out that accountant guy. He was jealous as hell over Kylo."

"Fred Thomas?" The accountant with the squinty eyes?

"Yeah, I know he looks all meek and mild, but he punched Kylo a couple days ago. He had it really bad for Zabrina."

A knock came on the front door. "Police. Open up."

ELEVEN

"How do I take my coffee? Pererably with Cassie." ~ Sanjay

Cassie and Sid materialized in Ophelia's attic, a room only accessible by magic. "I want to know who killed Zabrina. I haven't the patience to knock on everyone's door and listen to their dramas. And I'm a witch." Cassie ranted. She plunked herself down in the old swivel office chair behind the desk and stared at her crystal ball.

Sid walked across the desk and sat opposite her. "Really? Now? Bob?" She rolled her eyes and flicked her tail.

"Yes. Now. Why not? I need to use all of my resources."

"Because he's Bob." Sid's whiskers twitched.

"Hmph." Familiars could be so annoying.

"I hear your thoughts, you know," said Sid out loud, thumping her tail for emphasis.

Cassie floated her hand above the scrying ball and whispered an incantation. Light shone from within, and a green mist appeared around it.

"You called," said Bob, sounding much like a butler in a Munster movie.

Cassie gave Sid an all-knowing smile. "I call on the north, the south, the east, and the west. I call on the powers of the elements: water, earth, and sky. I call ..."

"What do you want?" said Bob. "I had a nice dream."

"I'm getting there."

"Uh-huh. Get there faster."

"Okay. Here's the deal. My friend, Zabrina Zafar, was murdered just before midnight. I want to see her death."

"Ewe. That's ghoulish even for you."

"Bob cut the commentary. Show me the scene."

He grunted. "I'm not a woogle map. That's a witch's google map for your information."

"Just help me, Bob."

An image of the town appeared in the center of the globe. "I need some help here. Where does she live?"

"Beside the docks."

"The image vanished, and another appeared, showing Orca Lane."

"Yes, that's it. Now go to the brick building near The Rusty Anchor pub."

The image flowed down the road to Zabrina's building, squeezing under the front door into her apartment and up the stairs to the crime scene. The blood on the bed had dried to an ugly dark crimson. Two policemen in bunny suits were taking measurements and plotting out the scene on paper. Gavin stood in the corner of the room with a worried expression.

"Now, can you go back in time?" asked Cassie.

Bob grunted a second time. "Listen to you—do this, do that. You sound more like a robot than a witch. Take a chill pill."

"Trust me, Bob. I'm all witch. Do as I command." With her words, the air in the room cooled, and the lights dimmed. What the fudge, thought Cassie. Obviously, The Perfect Brew agreed with her. Or her powers were growing. Or, both.

"You're powerful every day," mumbled Sid as she licked her paw.

"Testy. Testy," said Bob. "I'm working on it."

Zabrina's room turned dark. Light from the full moon slanted through her Venetian blinds. She lay asleep on the bed. The sound of footsteps on the staircase could be heard. Cassie's breath caught.

A towering figure dressed in a black sweat suit appeared at the landing with a knife in hand. They wore a hoody, and a scarf covered their nose and mouth. Night vision goggles encased their eyes. They strode towards Zabrina.

"Bob, can you zoom in on the murderer's face?"

The image faded and then became clearer, focusing on the killer's face. Cassie still couldn't see anything distinguishing about them.

"Okay, zoom out again and let me watch." She swallowed.

The murderer wasted no time. They walked to the side of the bed and plunged the knife into Zabrina's chest. As it broke her skin, she woke and screamed, but her life was over before she could do anything. Cassie took a deep breath.

SANJAY MATERIALIZED BESIDE THE DESK. "She didn't have a chance," he said.

Peregrine flew in and perched on his warlock's shoulder, clicking his beak.

"I agree with Peregrine. Your ability to see into the past is impressive, Cassie," said Sanjay.

"Do you have any news?" asked Cassie.

"No. I'm afraid not. The shifters chased the killer's scent all around town. It appears the murderer knew he or she would be followed and did a good job of leaving their scent everywhere. The wizards are studying images similar to Bob's."

Cassie took his hand. Her skin felt softer than silk. "I questioned Stardust," she said. "About the love triangle, she had going on with Zabrina and Kylo. It sounds messier than all hell, which, to my mind, gives her and Kylo a motive. But they have solid alibis. Stardust was singing at The Rusty Anchor to a full house, and Kylo was in the audience. I'll check it out, but I'm guessing lots of people saw both of them."

Sanjay kissed her hand. "I've got a meeting at the Keep with the Warriors in an hour. I'm hoping they'll know more by then."

"I'm going to have a chat with Fred Thomas."

"The accountant?"

"According to Stardust, he had feelings for Zabrina, and he's the jealous type."

"I did not know that." Sanjay pulled Cassie out of the chair and wrapped her in his arms. He kissed her deeply. "And how are you?"

"Besides having weak knees, I'm okay," she said.

He chuckled. "Honey, I have a cure for weak knees."

THE WAY HE SAID HONEY, melted Cassie's heart. "Oh, yeah." She knew all about his cures.

"Yeah. I'll make you feel weak all over, so your knees won't bother you so much."

Before she could comment, a flaming message shot through the air, and Sanjay caught it.

HE LET GO of her and read the message. His face paled. "My father's ill. I have to go."

TWELVE

"Bring on the brew." ∼ Jane

Jane opened the door to her new shop and sighed. "This is it. This is me. It feels so right. This is ..." Lifting her arms in the air, she danced.

Vixen used her paw to close the door, sat on her haunches, and watched.

"Vixen," Jane said, "this will be our place."

The cat mewed and tilted her round ginger face. She lifted her right paw in the air and waved it.

"Yes, I know Vixen, the Lord of Darkness is out there, but we're in here. That's what matters. The way I see it: I have two choices. I can sit and wait for Mr. Doom to appear, or carry on with my life despite him. I choose option two. I want to live. I want to love. I want to dance. I'm all for moving forward."

"Cassie won't approve," Vixen said in her soft voice.

"Of course not. She's my big sister. Big sisters never approve. The thing is, Cassie doesn't have visions. I do. This is my future, and it will help others."

Vixen strode over to the sunniest window and jumped up onto its ledge. "I like this spot," she said as she stretched out.

Cats, Jane thought. They get comfortable so quickly. It was a skill she would like to have. She rolled her suitcase to the side and breathed in the essence of the room. Yes, this would be her space. With salt, she drew a pentagram in the center on the floor and sat lotus-style in the middle. Silently she spoke the incantation from her vision, setting up protection wards and good-luck charms around and in the room.

She sensed more than heard Brody arrive outside. With a wave of her hand, she cleared her magical arena and went to the door to greet him.

Brody Buchanon, so perfect, but so taken. Tall, dark, and dangerously handsome did not begin to describe his alpha-male presence, and it pulled Jane like a magnet.

"Hey, Brody, thanks for coming."

"No problem." He strode into the storefront and looked around at the open space. "This is nice. It used to be the town's chocolate shop. I like it."

"Me too. It's got a good vibe."

He laughed at her. "If you say so."

"I do. I just need to add my own personality to it."

Brody nodded. "Ah. You've been reading the business books I gave you."

"Yup," she lied.

"I've got Gavin's truck. What do you want me to move? Let's get this done." His lopsided grin warmed her heart. Vixen put a paw over her eyes.

Jane pulled a list from her jean's pocket. "I thought we'd start with my desk and a new laptop."

As they opened the door, Gavin's classic, green sports car with a big Golden Retriever sitting in the passenger seat parked drove in. Gavin hopped out. "Hi, I thought I'd come by to see how you're doing."

"Are you spying on me, cousin?" asked Brody.

Gavin gave him a side glance; which Jane couldn't translate. Had to be a guy thing.

"Nope," said Gavin. "I just thought an extra set of arms might be useful."

"Don't you have a murder to deal with?" asked Jane.

"I'm on a break."

Brody glared at Gavin. "I'm just helping her move."

"I know that," said Gavin.

"I get it," said Jane. "Gavin's worried I'll kiss you."

"Yeah," said Brody. "He mentioned that. Is there something I should know?"

Gavin grimaced. "You put a ring on Sadie's finger. Is there anything else you need to know?"

Jane patted Gavin on his arm. "Don't worry. I won't trespass on your cousin."

Gavin lowered his eyes. "I don't want you bewitching him."

"Got it," said Jane, as she flicked her long red hair behind her shoulders and dramatically bathed her eyelashes.

"Uh-huh," said Gavin, folding his arms across his chest.

"How about I bewitch you?" she said.

"You guys are crazy," said Brody. "Let's get this work done."

"Okay, then," said Jane. "Gavin, we're heading to Watson's Office Surplus store to pick up my order. An extra set of strong arms would be most appreciated."

Gavin grumbled as he got back into his car, but he followed them down the road.

.   .   .

THIRTY MINUTES LATER, the parcels they collected had been moved to the storefront and opened. A desk with a new laptop and a large screen sat at one end of the room. Beside it, they placed a tall, old-fashioned, wooden filing cabinet. Jane didn't think she would ever use it as she had an excellent memory, but it looked good. They also lined up four comfortable office chairs along the east wall with a coffee table.

"It's a start," Jane said. "Thanks so much for your help. Both of you." She kissed each of them on the cheek and watched them blush in turn.

"I gotta go," said Gavin.

Jane reached into her purse and magically pulled out a thick roast beef sandwich on sourdough bread, wrapped in wax paper. She handed it to him. "Thanks for using your lunch break to help me out."

Gavin's right brow rose as she handed him his lunch. How did she know his favorite sandwich? Witches!

"It's okay. I didn't add a hex to the mayonnaise," she said.

"Right. Thank you." He grabbed Brody's left arm and pulled on him. "Your Mom said she wanted help with the boxes in the attic. I think you should be there."

"Later, Gavin," said Brody, who stood as immovable as a stone statue.

Once Gavin left, Brody turned to Jane. "Am I missing something?"

"Nope," lied Jane. "I don't think so."

Brody made a face. "I thought he was just worried about Sadie and me at first, but I'm beginning to think there's more to this scenario."

"About Sadie," said Jane, stepping closer to him.

"I told you the first time I met you. I'm engaged."

"Yeah, you did. But here's the thing. You don't act like a

man in love with another woman. That's what's bothering Gavin."

Brody looked up at the ceiling. His Adam's apple went up and then down again, but he said nothing.

"What aren't you telling me?"

"Sadie and I have been together for a long time. Everyone expects us to get hitched."

"And now you're wondering."

"Nope. Now I'm marrying."

Jane swallowed. "Is she pregnant?"

His brow beaded with sweat, and he looked towards the window but said nothing.

"She is, and you feel trapped, and you're wondering if you're going to miss out on something."

"It doesn't matter," he said. "It doesn't matter if I am or not. I'm marrying Sadie."

"If you don't love her, it will matter."

"I love her. I've loved her since grade five."

"So, what's the problem?"

He shrugged. "I gotta go."

THIRTEEN

"I understand obsessed coffee drinkers. I get thirsty myself."
~ Alessandro

Cassie sat with Sid on the sofa. "I don't know what Zabrina was thinking, or if she was thinking. Why would she let herself get involved in a love triangle?" She scratched the cat behind her ears. "They're messy as hex, and someone always gets hurt."

Sid stretched and yawned. "Look who's talking!"

Cassie gave Sid the stink eye. "I'm different."

Sid's whiskers twitched. "Three lovers make a triangle. When the mess fits, honey, own it."

"No. No way, Sid. I'm with Sanjay. There's just two of us in the relationship."

"I wonder what Alessandro would say about that?"

As if he heard his name, the vampire knocked on Cassie's second-floor window, as he hovered outside. She rushed to let him in. The last thing she needed was to have people see a giant of a man flying in the air outside her apartment.

"Oh, goodie," said Sid. "And the vampire makes three."

As Alessandro climbed inside, Cassie conjured a cup of cold water and poured it on her cat.

Sid screeched and ran from the room. "Own it, Cassie. Own it." Sid hissed. "You can't control the roll of the dice, but you can enjoy it."

Alessandro straightened to his full seven feet height and looked at Cassie. "Am I interrupting something?"

"No. But I really would prefer you to come to the front door."

His brows rose slowly. "And make a normal entrance!"

"Do I have to remind you? There are people in town who haven't a clue about supernaturals. I don't want to upset them."

The vampire grunted. "If you insist." He took her hand and bowed to kiss it. "I'm not here to fight with you, my cherished one. Unless, of course, you're in the mood for a little rough play."

Cassie tried hard not to smile. "Alessandro, how many times do I have to tell you that I'm with Sanjay."

Alessandro moved closer to her. "He is a handsome warlock. I could get used to him being around."

Cassie narrowed her eyes. "I don't want a ménage à trois. You know that."

"A pity. A devil's threeway would be fun." His eyes hardened to flints of stone, and he sighed. "I guess I'll have to kill him."

"Alessandro!"

He put his hand up to stop her from saying anything. "Just kidding. I know if I hurt him, I would never get you back. I want you back."

Cassie rubbed the spot between her eyes, where a

headache brewed. "I have things to do. Is there something I can do for you?"

"Sanjay is gone. Again."

"How do you know this?" Why did she even bother asking?

"I have spies. You know this about me."

"I am safe. That is all you need to know."

Alessandro walked around her. "You're more powerful now." He sniffed the air above her head. "But you know that, don't you?"

"Yes." There wasn't any point in lying to him.

"I find your magic alluring."

Sid walked back in the room, jumped up onto the couch, and purred.

Cassie fixed her eyes on Alessandro. "Don't use your vampire charm on me. It won't work."

The night stalker walked over to Sid and sat down beside her. He stroked her fur gently. "As much as I enjoy verbally sparring with you, Cassie, it's time we stopped playing games and really talked."

"I'm not playing games. I'm trying to live my life."

"You forget about us."

"There is no *us*. Can you not get that through your thick skull? We had a great run. I have wonderful memories of our five years together and no regrets. If you continue to hassle me over our break-up, I will regret the day I met you."

"Mmm. I remember that day. It was a beautiful spring morning in Paris. You wore a blue dress with thin straps, and your hair was long. It flowed over your bare shoulders. I thought I had never seen a woman look so vulnerable and so dangerous at the same time. You thought of yourself as a lousy witch, but you bewitched me the moment I met you. And when we made love that night ..."

"Stop it," she said. "Just stop it." She threw her arms in the air. "We're over."

"Ah, Cassie—sweet, sweet Cassie—that's not true."

"I love Sanjay."

The vampire growled. "That may be true for the moment. But you have a bond with me."

Her heart plummeted a haunted skyscraper. Veronica, her psychic witch friend, had told Cassie that she could see the bond, but Cassie hadn't believed her. She folded her arms. "When did that happen?"

"Remember our weekend in Venice?"

Images of their lover's retreat in a faded pink castle on the Grand Canal flew through her mind. "I remember taking the train to Venice. We ate amazing Italian meals, drank Tuscan wines, and went to the opera. I remember spending time in bed. A woman doesn't forget that kind of trip."

"You may recall ..." He hesitated. "I know you recall, we made love for hours on end, as if no one else in the world existed."

Cassie wanted to say no, but she wouldn't lie to him. "Yes, but that was then. So much has happened since."

"You may recall calling out my name."

"Yes." She remembered.

"And I used a bit of fang."

"So?" His teeth always showed up.

"So that's when I placed my bond on you. I did more than nip your neck that night. I placed a vampiric charm on your being."

More like a chain! "Without my consent? You never even told me? How dare you."

"Now. Now. Calm down."

"Is it permanent?"

"As you slept in my arms, I whispered a vampire incantation to prepare you to seal our union. That is all."

"I don't want to be sealed."

"You didn't mind that night. You may recall the sex got better and better."

That she did. Darn, the dead man. "Is it permanent?"

"I planned to tell you when the time was right."

"Is. It. Permanent?"

"But life happens, and I never got around to talking to you about it."

"I thought vampires bonded with other vampires if they bonded at all."

"Well, yes and no. We are all different, you know. Our present bond will become fully actualized when you cross over from the mortal realm and become one of us. Then we will be eternal mates." He said all of this as if he was reading the menu at the local Micky Dees as if the details were not at all extraordinary.

Anger boiled in Cassie's gut. Her chest tightened, her cheeks burned, and her magic swirled. She got up and paced the floor. "I do not want to be a vampire. I've told you that a million times."

"Yes, my love. But you will age, and as you age, the beauty of eternal life will seem more enchanting."

Enchanting! "So that's it. You want a mate who is not only a vampire but a vampire- witch. That's the real reason you chose me." Her anger grew, and the lights in the room flashed on and off.

Alessandro tilted his head back. "I admit, you being a witch adds to your package."

Package! Could she kill him? Was her magic strong enough to strike him permanently dead? She would have to decapitate him. But she was mad enough to manage that with a butter knife. Or maybe she should just castrate him. Ah, yes. That would feel good.

"Calm down, Cassie. You don't look well."

"I can't believe what a fool I've been." She shook her head. "I thought you loved me."

The vampire stood and walked towards her. "In my own way, I do love you, Cassie. You will learn to understand that vampires experience love differently."

"More practically."

"Well, yes, you could say that. We are old, after all."

Time for a new approach. "So, our bond will be complete after you turn me."

"Correct." He gathered her in his strong arms and pulled her to his rock-hard chest. She could smell his charm, his sense of adventure ... his death, and it left her cold. Pushing him away, she shivered.

"Then it's not binding yet. It's a loose bond."

He stroked her hair. "It's my pledge to you and our love."

"Okay, then. I refuse."

He stared at her. "You can't refuse me."

"I just did."

"I am Alessandro of Amsterdam. You ..."

"I am Cassie, the witch." Drawing magic from every cell of her body, she focused it in her mind and threw it at him. A crackling current of blue light shot from her hands lifted the vampire into the air and threw him against the wall. His body made a loud "whack" sound when it hit. "I will not be your mate, now or ever. Know this, Alessandro: our bond is done."

Alessandro fell to the ground in a heap laughing. "We'll see about that," he said. In a black swirl of energy, he shifted into a giant bat and flew out the open window.

FOURTEEN

"According to chemists, coffee is a solution."
~ Anonymous

After spending a useless hour licking wounds and counting miseries, Cassie decided to refocus her energy. There would be time to deal with *the fangman* later, preferably after she talked with Sanjay. For now, she had a killer to catch. It was the only thing she could do for Zabrina.

Outside, the weather had turned drizzly. A gray mist blanketed the town, and Cassie could see only six feet in front of her. Crows collected on telephone lines watching everyone. If she had to think of one word to describe the day, it would be creepy. Real creepy. Edgar Allan Poe creepy.

Cassie and Sid arrived at Fred Thomas's office on the main street two blocks south of The Brew at four o'clock. It was a turn of the last century, red-brick building. A sign hung above his door, "Fred J. Thomas, Chartered Accountant."

As they entered, bells tinkled.

The waiting room lined with five chairs looked as inviting as a dentist's office. The coffee table displayed an assortment of popular magazines organized in three neat piles. At the far end of the room, a receptionist sat behind a well-organized desk. A young woman with a long face and large oval glasses, she stared at the witch.

"Hi, I'm Cassie ..."

"Black," the receptionist said, finishing Cassie's sentence. "Everyone knows about you and your family."

Okay then. "Have we met?"

The young woman sighed and leaned back. "No. I'm Sadie Sugarman. I'm engaged to Brody Buchanan."

Cassie smiled and nodded, but her name didn't really connect. Had Jane mentioned her?

"Gavin MacGregor's cousin," the receptionist added.

"Oh!" Jeez, Louise! Everyone in this town is related to Gavin, "How wonderful. Congratulations on your engagement."

Sadie's lips pursed as if she wanted to say something, but stopped herself. Not a good look on anyone.

Cassie waited a few seconds hoping she would spit it out, but when she didn't, Cassie proceeded with her own agenda. "I'd like a word with Mr. Thomas, if possible." She marveled at how such a young woman could command such a strong presence.

"He doesn't have an appointment for ten minutes, but he may be too busy with paperwork to see you." Her grey eyes simmered.

Cassie looked at the ceiling. What had she done to this woman? Wait, maybe the question was, what had someone in the family done to this woman? "Could you ask Mr. Thomas?" she said.

Sadie tossed her head, sending her ponytail swaying, and typed a message to her boss. She frowned.

Cassie sighed.

"You can go in," Sadie said and didn't grace her with eye contact. "He said he would see you right now."

The worry line on Fred Thomas's brow had not moved since she had last seen him. He stood when she entered and shook her hand with a firm grip. "Good to see you, Cassie. Good to see you. Very good to see you. What can I do for you?"

He wore a well-cut business suit with a white shirt and striped blue tie. Gel held his short hair in place, and his breath smelled of mouth wash. He motioned for her to sit.

"I'm sure you've heard the news."

He frowned. "Yes. I heard Zabrina died last night. I am sorry for your loss. I know you were good friends. She mentioned you often."

"Yes, we liked to talk about art."

"And men. Did you talk, men?"

"Excuse me?"

"Oh, sorry. I suck at small talk. I guess. I hoped. I don't know. I ..."

He hesitated for a few seconds. "I liked Zabrina. And I had hoped she might have mentioned me."

"I'm sorry for your loss," Cassie said.

He nodded. "Thank you. Zabrina was so full of life. Not like any woman I ever met." He looked down at the blotter on his desk. "You would never think someone like her would want to spend time with me, a dull number-cruncher, but she did. It was a miracle. She didn't put people in boxes." He sighed. "We used to watch old movies together on Wednesday nights. I'd bring a baguette and a bottle of good wine. She would put together a plate of cheese and meats. We would laugh and sometimes cry together. They were golden times. I once asked her why she hung out with me when she could be with so many other men. She told me it was the kindness in my soul that drew her. But I think the kindness was in her soul. I will miss her."

Cassie felt her heart lighten. That was so Zabrina. "We were both lucky to have her in our lives," she said.

He cleared his throat. "Zabrina was an exceptional woman. I thought of her as an angel in my life."

Cassie nodded.

"Occasionally, she would call me out of the blue, just to say good morning and tell me about catching the sunrise. I never really looked at sunrises before I met her. Zabrina saw beauty in life."

"She was the beauty in life," Cassie said.

Fred straightened his back and looked at Cassie directly. "Enough about me and my grief. What can I do for you? I'd do anything to help a friend of Zabrina's."

Cassie took a breath. "I want to find her murderer. I heard the two of you were close, and I thought you might have some ideas." It sounded lame when she said it out loud.

"We were just friends, but good friends. I hoped someday she would see me as more, but I don't think that would ever have happened. She liked a different sort of man. Women go for the bad-boy types."

"Do you think one of those men could have killed her? I'm grasping at straws here."

Fred picked up a pen and tapped it on his desk. "You know about her love triangle, right? Stardust, Kylo, and her."

"I heard you punched Kylo."

Fred frowned. "You would have done the same if you heard what he said about Zabrina at the bar."

"Oh?"

"Yeah. Let's just say the Italian creep doesn't understand the gentleman's code."

"He talked about ..."

"Their sex life, in detail, or at least his version of it."

"Ah. I see. And that made you mad?"

"I've never felt so angry. Zabrina was making love with him, but all he's capable of is collecting the experience as another victory in a sad story of conquests."

"What did he say?" She had to ask. The details might help.

"Gross stuff, like which positions turned her on, the sounds she made, and how much she liked it rough, and ..."

Cassie put her hand up. "Okay, that's enough for me."

Fred shook his head. "The guy always brags about his latest. According to him, he's bedded almost every available woman in town. I bet he makes half of the stuff up from watching porn movies. I bet that's all he really does during the day." Fred leaned back. "So, I called him an asshole, told him what I really thought of him." Fred smiled. Kylo came at me, swinging."

"Good for you," Cassie said, smiling at the image of the mild-spoken accountant fighting for Zabrina's honor.

"Botticelli threw one punch towards my face and missed before Gavin broke us up. He got sent to jail for fighting in a public place, and I got sent home." He thumped his pen. "I got the impression Gavin had heard enough of his stories, as well."

"It's hard to imagine women want to spend time with that creep." But then Cassie remembered how that creep looked in boxers. "I'm glad you took him down a peg."

"Thanks." He huffed out a breath. "Is there anything else I can do for you?"

"Can you tell me where you were last night between eleven and twelve?"

He nodded. "Playing poker with friends. My alibi is solid." He scribbled on a piece of paper. "These are the names of five of the players. Feel free to check on me. I'll do whatever it takes to help you find the killer."

Cassie smiled. "Please, don't be offended. I'm checking everyone out." She took the piece of paper and stood. "How did you meet Zabrina?"

"She came to me for help on a project." He looked at the window and then back at Cassie. "Mystic Arts, she called it, a gallery-slash-art-studio, where creatives could work together and sell their art. She wanted my opinion on the numbers she had come up with for her business plan."

"Were they sound?"

He exhaled noisily. "If Zabrina could get the government and private grants she applied for, it would have been sufficiently funded to start. Over time she would have had to generate revenue from it, but that probably wouldn't be a problem as tourists love to collect our local art."

"It would have been great."

"Come to think of it, Zabrina was upset yesterday about one of the private grants. A man by the name of Mullins was pulling out. She said it was because she had refused to sleep with him. I could get his information for you."

"Yes, please, that would be great."

Cassie's cell phone rang. What the hex? Thought Cassie. No one ever calls me. She clicked on the call.

"Cassie, it's me." Oscar's voice. "We need you at The Brew."

FIFTEEN

"Today, my coffee needs a coffee."
~ Coffee Fuels The World Meme, Facebook

"I gotta go," Cassie said to the accountant over her shoulder as she rushed for the door. Outside she broke into a run. Conjuring a portal amid all the people on Main Street would be too revealing. Sanjay would have the power to cloak such an action, but she couldn't. She had to trust her feet.

Two storefronts down from The Perfect Brew, she ran into what felt like a brick wall. Dazed, she stepped back. A seven-foot monster of a man, wearing jeans and a down jacket appeared before her. His square face looked small above his stocky build, and the glare of his black eyes, soul-less orbs from hell, sent a shiver up her spine. "The Black witch," he said.

Where the hex had he come from? Cassie looked around, but the surroundings muted to a blurred landscape. She could see the shapes of people and buildings, but no details. It was as if she stood in a white-washed world of reality. What the hex?

"I'm here. This is happening," said Sid in a hiss as she shifted into her full panther form.

The giant swung picked up Sid's changling form and threw it high into the air. Cassie didn't watch her familiar land but felt her cat's pain in her own body.

Without thought, Cassie attacked. Sanjay's boring fight lessons had finally come in handy. Rule number one was to not wait to be attacked. She could see no way of avoiding the brute, so she had to take him on.

Whispering a spell to strengthen her powers, she raised both her arms and sent fire through the air. It stopped six inches from the villain's body, hitting an invisible protective shield, and slid to the ground where it evaporated into smoke.

He chuckled. "Is that all you've got?'

She took a deep breath and screamed as loudly as she could. But the sound bounced back at her.

The monster swung his right arm towards her, and she used her magic to avoid his blow. His arms swung at her again and again. Each time, her body shifted just in the nick of time. How long could she avoid his blows? He had her on the defense. It was taking all her energy to stay alive. One wrong slip and he would have her. She needed to change the course of events.

He stepped closer. Cassie jumped back and felt the edge of the invisible prison Erebus had cast around them. Unable to move further away from the beast, she breathed in his stench, a mixture of putrid meat used in the conjuring of form and black magic.

In stories, kickass heroines always made great plans at moments like this, but Cassie's mind went blank. All she could think about was Sanjay and how she wouldn't get to spend the rest of her life with him, wouldn't get to have his child, wouldn't get to make a home with him. Images of Sid and her family flew through her mind. Never again would she get to hang out with her sisters. It wasn't fair. Her life shouldn't be cut so short.

She looked for Sid. The cat's form lay still on the ground, but Cassie detected a faint sign of life within her.

"Not so frisky now, eh?" The beast folded his arms. "Some witch you are."

Cassie's pulse raced. At least he had stopped trying to hit her. Her chest felt tight as if it was squeezed by the devil himself, and the rest of her body felt leaden with dread. She reached into her purse and pulled out her hairbrush. Spelling it with speed, she hurled it at the ogre between his eyes. It made a thudding sound when it hit. He took a step back.

The monster growled and swore, and for a moment, Cassie felt hope. She pulled out a makeup mirror and repeated the spell, aiming her weapon at his knees. He wouldn't expect that. She threw it like a Ninja in a cartoon.

Blood gushed from his wound, and he yelled out in pain.

Next, Cassie pulled out a tube of lipstick and sent it flying into his right eye.

Swiping at the missive in the air, her assailant growled so loud the ground trembled. But he didn't catch her weapon. It hit him in the center of his right eye. That was a sight she instantly wished she had never seen. The tube moved with such force it penetrated his brain and flew out the other side of his head. There was blood. Lots of blood.

As he screamed in agony, he doubled over in pain.

Donovan O'Reilly materialized beside her with his

sword drawn. He took one look at the beast, one look at her and sheathed his weapon. His lips quirked up on one side. "Well done, Cassie."

Her pulse slowed, and her senses calmed. A weird sense of pride for besting a beast flowed through her consciousness. It felt oddly satisfying. Its death was necessary. Slowly she exhaled a breath she had been holding.

It was over. The terror. The fear. The exhilaration. The kill. It was all over. She couldn't believe that she had bested the beast.

Donovan took one step forward and beheaded the monster with a single stroke of his warlock's sword. The assailant's remains ignited into a blue flame. Clearly, he had never been human.

With her next breath, Cassie stood tall. She had survived.

Never again would she take her life, or the people she loved, for granted. Not one of them. Ever. It might have been only a moment in time, but the fight had changed her profoundly, and she felt it in the very fiber of her being.

"I wonder how long that will last," murmured Sid, who had returned to her housecat form and materialized beside her. "I give it a week." She licked at her bloody shoulder.

"Sid!" She picked her up. "Are you okay?"

"You know me, Cassie. I always land on my feet."

Cassie stroked the cat's fur, matted with blood.

"Cassie." Donovan's gravelly voice drew her attention.

She turned towards him. "Thanks, Donovan, for coming to my rescue. How did you know I needed you?"

His lips quirked up again.

"Oh, I knew. We all knew." He continued to beam at her. "All sorts of alarms went off. First, the wizards alerted me that a time-warp bubble had appeared on Main Street. Then Sid arrived bleeding at the steps of The Keep."

"And then?" Cassie could tell there was more to the story.

"Then, I could feel deep magic, powerful magic, flow through town. I knew something significant was happening. I guessed that you, a Pur Dei, were fighting for your life."

"I appreciate your support," she said.

"Hmm." Donovan took her by the shoulders and looked down at her with his Irish blue eyes. "You did fine, this time, Cassie. Very fine."

"Hex, yeah!" raved Sid. "She walloped the bastard of a beast."

Donovan shook his head. "Next time, Erebus may send more than one. Could you take on two? Or three? How about an army?"

What a delightful thought. Talk about a party killer. "I'll deal with whatever, whenever. That's all I can do," Cassie said.

"Hmm."

Urgh. Not for the first time, Cassie couldn't fathom the warlock. Donovan O'Reilly was so devastatingly handsome people swooned in his presence. He was so skilled in the art of warfare, warriors bowed to him. The man had serious mojo. None the less, he couldn't talk worth a darn. Why couldn't he express himself with words? "What the hex does, 'Hmmmmmmmmmmm' mean?" she asked.

"You need more training."

"Sure. I'll add it to my to-do list. Right now, I have to get to The Brew. Something's wrong."

SIXTEEN

"May your burdens be light and your coffee strong." ~
Koffee Addict meme, Facebook

The antique clock struck three, as Cassie and Sid appeared inside The Perfect Brew. Donovan arrived a second later. Oscar stood behind the coffee bar cradling something wrapped in a towel.

"What happened," asked Cassie.

"I'm not sure. The house called me at my apartment thirty minutes ago and said I had to return. I found this bundle on the doorstep.

"The house? You mean The Perfect Brew?" said Donovan. They all knew the coffee house was sentient, but for the most part, she remained silent.

He nodded.

Sid jumped onto the bar and sniffed the air.

"I'm afraid to ask," said Cassie.

"It's Zoey," said Oscar

Cassie gasped. "The Zoey!" Ophelia's familiar? She had heard too many stories to count about this cat who had accompanied Ophelia through her many adventures. "Let me see."

Oscar pulled back. "I don't think you want to see her."

"She's been spelled," said Donovan. Cassie could feel it too.

"She appears unharmed, but I can't get her to wake up. I've used every spell I know, but she seems to be in some kind of comma. I've sent for our healers," said Oscar.

"Why aren't you letting us see her?" asked Cassie.

Sid let out a plaintive yowl.

"I smell evil," said Donovan.

Oscar's eyes welled with tears. "I spent a lot of time with Zoey."

"Oscar." Cassie pressed.

"Zoey isn't like any other familiar I've known. She has a big heart and a kickass sense of humor. She loves telling stories. Like her mistress, she enjoyed life to the fullest. And she ..." His voice trailed for a moment. "She really knew how to love."

Sid's tail twitched.

Cassie and Donovan walked around the bar to get closer to Oscar. They each touched one of his arms as he rocked Zoey.

"Oscar," said Cassie.

"Not yet," he said.

"Oscar?"

Mumbling a prayer, he closed his eyes for a minute and held the familiar's body tight. Slowly he handed his bundle over to Cassie, who placed her on the bar. Donovan opened the blanket.

Cassie's scream rocked the room. The lights in the coffee house flashed in response, and the floor trembled. Zoey had a pulse, but her body appeared frozen.

"Erebus is sending us another message," said Donovan.

"Darkness is coming," said Oscar.

"No." Cassie shook her head. "Darkness is here." Cassie's heart leaped into her throat. As her tears fell freely, she thanked the universe that Ophelia did not have to witness this horror. Surely the healers would have spells that could fix her.

The front door of The Brew burst open and slammed into the wall. Alessandro strode into the room. "What happened?" he said.

Donovan drew his sword and pulled magic to his weapon. Oscar stood very still.

"What happened, my cherished one?" the vampire repeated. "Something is wrong. I know this. I felt you fight for your life, and then I felt your deep sorrow. What happened?"

Where should she start? She looked at Zoey's still body.

Alessandro followed her gaze and sniffed the air. "The Dark Lord."

Cassie nodded. "It's Ophelia's cat. We thought she ran away. Some familiars do that, to mourn their witch. Sometimes they reappear. Sometimes they don't. We didn't look for her. We just assumed she was all right."

"Someone left Zoey on our doorstep," said Oscar. He stared at the vampire. "We can handle this, bloodsucker. We don't need your help."

"Oscar's right," said Donovan in a commanding voice. "We do not want you here, night stalker."

"Sanjay is not here." Alessandro hissed. His fangs descended. "He left Cassie alone. Again."

"I am here," said Oscar, "and I will protect her with my life."

"And, I am always at her command," said Donovan.

Cassie growled. "Good gravy-grief. I'm right here, boys. I'm a witch, fully capable of protecting myself." The lights in the room flickered, and the sound of thunder rumbled in the distance. She hadn't meant to let magic escape her body, but the effect was kinda cool, like an echo of her feelings.

Alessandro's right brow rose. "The witch in you is growing stronger, my darling one."

"Yes," she replied. "You better watch out." Her words sounded harsh, but her heartfelt like mush spinning in a clothes dryer.

She walked to the front entrance. When she opened the door, cold air flowed inside, calming her mood. The low winter sunlight gave the landscape a hazy sheen. A dozen or so people walked along the street. She bit her lip. Outside, life continued as usual. A young couple walked a golden retriever on a leash. They chatted with one another as if no one else in the world mattered. Imelda, a witch friend who always won at poker, waved at Cassie from the other side of the street before she disappeared into the candle store. Nothing looked out of the ordinary. That was the worst of it, thought Cassie. The town looked peaceful, like a place filled with goodness, but evil lurked within it. She continued to hold the door, hoping Alessandro would take the hint.

The vampire walked up behind her. "We need to talk." His cold presence felt familiar, but the prickly sensation that ran up and down her spine was far new.

"What is it you're not telling me?" she said as she turned to face him. "I don't have time to play games. Just tell me."

"We must be alone," he said.

"No. Way." Oscar's voice boomed. "I'm not letting that happen on my watch."

"Mmm," mumbled Donovan.

"She is safe with me," the vampire said. "I love her, like no other."

"Says the bloodsucker." Oscar lifted his arms to fight. Flames grew in his hands.

Cassie felt an eye-roll coming on, but she stopped herself. "Enough. I will go upstairs with Alessandro for an hour. If I need anyone's help, I'll let you know."

"Keep the door open," said Oscar.

Donovan nodded. "I will return to The Keep. Call me if I am needed."

Sid purred as she followed Cassie up the stairs.

Once inside her apartment, Alessandro walked to her window and looked outside for signs of trouble. His eyes blazed as he moved stealthily around the perimeter of the main floor, a vampire on the hunt. He returned to Cassie, who sat at her kitchen table.

"We are safe," he declared.

"What the hex, Alessandro?" she said.

"I don't want you alone. I love you. You are mine. I must keep you safe. Have I not made myself clear?" His low voice rumbled through the room.

"Crystal clear. But I'm with Sanjay."

"Why did Sanjay leave this time?"

"Family stuff," she said.

"Why did you not go with him?" he said.

Cassie sighed. "I wasn't asked. I'm guessing I wouldn't fit into the warlock world any better than I fit into yours."

"I don't like this." The vampire grumbled.

"I can see that. But what else is bothering you."

His eyes calmed, and for a moment, he looked almost human. "I want you, Cassie."

She exhaled noisily. "How many times do I have to tell you? I'm with Sanjay."

"That young warlock cannot give you what I can give you." He gave a strangled vampire growl. "You have what I want, and I have what you need."

That sounded like a really lousy pick-up line. "I'm tired," Cassie said. "I'm angry. I'm hurting. I have no patience left." Cassie ran a hand through her hair. "I was attacked earlier." She told him about the beast and grunted through her whole tale.

When she finished, he said, "Sanjay should have been here."

"You've already said that." Cassie sighed. "I know there is something else that's bothering you. Let's get to the truth."

"The truth?" Alessandro's brow rose.

"Tell me more about our binding." She couldn't think of any other reason for him to be so bothered.

Alessandro looked towards the windows. "You are not fully bound to me." He turned back to stare into her eyes. "Yet."

"But?"

He folded his arms. "The bond I placed on you is more like an intention, like an engagement ring, as opposed to a wedding ring."

Should she throw a book at him? The fridge would hurt more. "You didn't ask my permission. And I will not give it."

"No, I did not. I didn't need your permission. I didn't tell you because I knew it would upset your modern woman's sense of independence." He made a face, the one he often made when we watched Romcom movies. "You have to understand. I bound you to protect you. As my lover, you were exposed to other vampires, but once bound, you became off-limits."

"Am I to feel like a piece of prime meat?"

Alessandro growled. "More like territory. You don't understand. You're not even trying to understand. I feared another vampire could take you and use you. I couldn't have that."

"How gallant of you." Her stomach flipped.

"I love you, Cassie. In my own way, I truly, love you."

Alessandro had never used the l-word before, but it wasn't enough, and it was way too late. "Does this intention ring have an expiration date?" Like yogurt, she thought.

A grin pulled on the right side of his mouth. "It lasts until my final bond is placed upon you and sealed with our coupling. It would, I might add, involve a long, hot night of sex and blood lust, more erotic than anything your mind can imagine."

Now he sounded like an info-commercial. "And if the binding is not made final?"

Alessandro growled, and the fine lines around his eyes hardened. "We are meant to be together, my cherished one. Give me another chance. If you let me bring you over, I would need no other woman, ever."

And there it was. "You bloodsucking fool. How could you ever think I would want to be dead?"

"Living-dead. It is not dead," he said solemnly. "Vampires have a life filled with pleasure. Let me introduce you to it."

The info-commercial again. Cassie felt his vampire charm pulling on her senses, but her guards would not let it in. "No way," she said. Anger brewed in her gut. "Take it off me."

Alessandro leaned back, and his vampire charm melted away. "Alas, there is no need to do anything."

Cassie narrowed her eyes.

"In memory of all you have meant to me, all you still

mean to me, I will be perfectly honest with you. Your growing witch-power is burning through the ring. It's evaporating as if it were nothing—as if our time together, our love —is nothing."

"That's why you keep coming back."

"Yes. I have come to plead with you."

"I understand. But how did you know I was in trouble?"

"Honey, I will always know." His voice sounded sadder than a dog with no moon to howl at. "It's a blood thing. I have your blood within my heart.

A chill ran through Cassie's veins. Great, just peachy-great. Amid the chaos, she needed to console the heart of an old lover without giving him any hope of ever having her again.

"Let me make love to you one last time."

Sid purred.

SEVENTEEN

"Coffee makes my world go round." ~ Oscar

Meanwhile, in a dimension far, far away ...

Sanjay sat on the cold, dirt floor of his dungeon cell. Chains made with black magic bound his feet and hands. After spending hours fighting the forces that held him, prisoner, he gave up. Some mighty, rogue warlock, he thought. How could he be so easily captured?

Refusing to give in, he reviewed his situation for the hundredth time.

Four brick walls. No windows. One wooden door that never opened.

No escape.

A family of rats nested in the corner munching on bones and gristle that looked vaguely human and smelled vile.

No light.

No sound, except for the relentless dripping of water seeping out of the walls, and of course, the rats.

What had he done?

He should have been more careful. He should have been prepared. He shouldn't have been so stupid. He ....

Self-recriminating thoughts played in his mind over and over again, like a vinyl record with a scratch. If his father had indeed been sick, his mother would have contacted him, not The Brotherhood. He should have known that. He should have detected the lie. He had let himself get so carried away with his new life, with Cassie ... with happiness and the threat of the Dark Lord, that he had been captured. Some warrior-warlock he was! He swore at himself.

Whoever sent him here, knew him well. He had been living in fear of his father having a second heart attack, so when he got the instant flame message, he didn't question it. He headed home.

Three, black hell-hounds intercepted him as he attempted to enter the warlock hospital where he figured his father was hospitalized. They jumped him and held him in the ether, as their leader, sank her teeth into his leg. He lost consciousness. When he awoke, he found himself here, in a tomb worse than every level of hell.

How long had it been? Stilling his mind, he sought an answer. A day, maybe two? It depended on how long he had been out cold. With him gone, Cassie was vulnerable. That was the worst of it.

He cursed himself again, and again, and cursed the rats for good measure. What kind of warlock left his woman undefended?

Taking a deep breath in, he exhaled slowly and concentrated on his options. He surveyed the room for the millionth time, and for the million-and-oneth time, he found no escape. Calming his mind to a pinprick of energy, he reached out to Cassie, but he couldn't make a connection.

In turn, he tried Oscar and O'Reilly, but couldn't reach them either. Finally, he put a distress call out to The Brotherhood, but the sound of his lament echoed back into his own ears. The dark enchantments placed on the dungeon prevented him from communicating.

No escape. No communication. What next?

Sleep. Sanjay told himself he should rest and be ready for whatever came next, but sleep would not come.

A day later, the old wooden door creaked open, and a seven-foot-tall figure emerged, cloaked in a cape made of dragon skin that glowed purple, pink, and silver in the darkness. In his hand, he held a torch.

"Brackenfeld! I should have known it." Sanjay said as he sat up.

"You had to know that I would even the score eventually," the older warlock said, as he pulled back his hood and revealed his hardened face, framed by a long mane of white hair. His most distinguishing feature was the jagged scar crossing his left cheek, the mark left by Sanjay's magic.

"Go to hell," Sanjay said and spit on the ground. "You have no right to detain me. When The Warlock Brotherhood hears of this, you will be banished."

The giant of a man walked closer to Sanjay and chuckled. "Haven't you heard? I already am banished, thanks to you opening up an investigation about my behavior with women."

He kicked Sanjay's foot, hard enough to make him wince.

"It's all your doing." Thomas Brakenfeld gave a deep growl, a menacing sound only the older warlocks made. "Everything that has gone wrong in my life is your doing."

"As if your legendary cruelty had nothing to do with it?" said Sanjay.

"How I treated Arianna was none of your business, then or now. A man sometimes has to put his wife in her place. Something you would have learned had you taken the time to marry."

Sanjay narrowed his eyes. "You beat Arianna repeatedly. She was sixteen. You were decades older."

"The wench was a reluctant learner." The older warlock sneered down at Sanjay. "How's your woman doing? I hear she's a tasty-looking, witchy."

Sanjay rolled his eyes. How he hated it when men talked about women as if they were livestock, or worse, whores.

"I'd like to have a taste of her. Take her for a good ride." Noting Sanjay's unruffled expression, his brows rose. "Do you doubt my intention? Perhaps I will have you watch me. Watch her die."

Sanjay swallowed the bile rising in his throat. "What do you want from me, Brackenfeld?"

"Your pain," Brackenfeld answered. "Your pain will do nicely. I want to watch you hurt, and then I want you to hurt more. You cannot escape from this place. I made it just for you. Your own cozy prison, complete with hungry rats, tucked between dimensions in a place no one will ever find. Even if they come looking—and I don't think they will—they won't find you. You are alone, and you will suffer."

Sanjay pulled at his chains, but they didn't budge. Blood trickled from his wrists. He pulled some more.

Brackenfeld walked the length of the cell. "Trouble is brewing in your hometown. I thought you should know that. The trouble will keep Cassie and your friends too busy to worry about you." He chuckled. "And I hear a certain vampire wants to take your place. So, you see. It's just you, and me, and time. That is all you have now. Time to regret your mistakes. Time to feel pain."

Sanjay's anger rolled in his gut, but he said nothing.

Brackenfeld towered above him. "How do you think Cassie would like a good, solid whipping?"

EIGHTEEN

"Today's good mood is sponsored by coffee."
~ Oscar

Jane woke the next day to the smell of Alessandro in the apartment. She smiled. Cassie had more than her share of men. A warlock, a vampire and a cop; a triple shot of trouble, Jane thought, or the beginning of a terrible joke. It was high drama, and so much dirt to share with her sisters back home.

Dressing in her favorite pair of jeans and a skinny, black tee-shirt, she felt ready. Despite all the talk of doom and gloom at The Brew, she planned to have a great day. Her shop was almost ready.

Jane had never been one to look on the dark side of things. Sanjay would return, and Cassie would smile again. Together they would take on Erebus. She was sure of all of that.

Alessandro would eventually give up on trying to give Cassie back and move on with his life. Gavin, she figured, already had.

Pulling a hand through her tangle of long red curls, she stared at herself in the mirror. Her loving, white magic was just what Mystic Keep needed. Others may doubt her, but she knew her vision to be true. Her business, "Dial-a-Witch," would make the locals very happy.

Alessandro hissed as she entered the kitchen where he squared-off with her sister.

"Nice to see you too," Jane said with a smirk.

"He's just passing through," said Cassie.

Jane looked at Alessandro, a picture of masculine, supernatural perfection with fangs. Hard muscles, smoldering sensuality, and a killer smirk. A trifecta of seduction. She sighed. If only he wasn't dead.

The vampire narrowed his eyes. "Ignore your sister. I'm staying."

Jane stifled an eye roll. "Of course," she said. "Of course, you are. Well, Alessandro, the coffin Sanjay conjured for you, is still at the bottom of my cupboard. The sun ..."

"I know little one. The sun is breaking the horizon. I am a vampire."

The way he said *vampire* chilled her bones and thrilled her nether parts. He certainly was—all vampire. Jane tossed her hair behind her shoulders and headed for the coffee pot. "Yeah. Your fangs kind of gave that away." She emptied yesterday's coffee from her Press into the sink. "You know, Alessandro, if you want me to root for you in this love triangle thing, you should be nicer to me." She turned on the tap. "Or, I guess it's a rectangle, of sorts."

"It's not geometry." Alessandro hissed. "It's love. Cassie is my *woman*."

The way he said 'woman' hit Jane in the female parts like a grenade. Wouldn't it be nice to have a man who referred to you like that? She cleared her throat. "I don't think she sees it that way."

Cassie's face turned bright red, and her hands shook. Pointing her index finger at Alessandro, she said, "I. Am. My. Own. Woman." The words stuttered out through gritted teeth. "You are so infuriating." It had been a long night of arguments.

The vampire's eyes gleamed with naughty thoughts, and his smile hitched on one side.

Jane looked at Alessandro, and then at Cassie. The air between them filled with anger and frustration, but also with an undeniably hotter-than-hades sexual tension. Jane put her French Press down carefully on the counter. "I'll get my coffee downstairs," she said.

Locked in a passionate tryst of love and hate, neither of the former lovers noticed, as Jane vanished to the ground floor.

WHEN JANE GOT to her store later, with a take-out brew in hand, she found Brody sitting in his brother's truck out front. He opened the door and jumped to the ground. Six feet of blue-eyed, country boy, complete with dimples. The day was getting better.

"I thought I'd help you, seeing as it's your first day," he said.

First day! At least someone remembered. This was the first day she officially owned her business. "That's nice of you," she said. She swallowed a lump of excitement growing in her throat.

"I could help you move furniture, or put up more signs, or just hang out."

"Uh-huh," Jane said. "Come on in."

He held her coffee as she fumbled with keys. Of course, if he hadn't been so close, she would have just used magic to open the door. They gained entry, and he followed her over to her office desk. She motioned for him to sit in one of the guest chairs.

Like a puppy dog, he did as she instructed.

Jane walked around the room for a couple minutes deciding on how best to talk to him and then sat cross-legged on the floor in front of him. "Brody, we need to talk."

"It's a beautiful day," he said.

And it was. The sun had burned through the morning mist and looked to be staying around for a while. A good thing, in the Pacific Northwest, she thought. The week of rain had seemed endless, and she wasn't sure she would ever adapt to the weather.

"I agree, but Brody, we need to talk."

He looked down at his boots. "I know," He inhaled deeply. "I know I've been giving you mixed messages, talking about my engagement one minute, and flirting the next.

Jane's brows rose. "Well, what I wanted to say is that I appreciate all the support you've given me as a friend to set up my business." She gave him her mega-watt smile. "But I want to make it clear that we are just friends. In another world, in another time, we may have been more. I won't deny my attraction to you. It's been fun, flirting. But right here, right now, we are friends. I hope you invite me to your wedding."

He smiled wide enough for his dimple to come out. "Your friendship is important to me," he said.

"You said I'm interfering with your relationship with your fiancé. That's not right. That's just not right. You've pledged your heart and your life to your fiancé." How could she say this without really muddling things up, like she usually did? "You are a hot guy, but you are not for me, and I am not for you."

His brows collided like tanks in a war. "Uh, do I have a say in this? I'm not married yet."

"Brody, you need to sort yourself out. If you aren't committed to your girlfriend, why are you marrying her? If you take me out of the equation, do you feel more certain of your feelings for her."

"I love Sadie. I know that. It's the marriage thing that makes me nervous." The truth of his words shone in his eyes.

"Maybe you're not ready for that step," said Jane.

"She's two months pregnant."

Jane took a deep breath. "So, you're doing what you think is the right thing to do. You're standing by her."

He leaned back. "We've been together since fifth grade."

"You've never been with another woman?"

"I've never wanted to until I met you."

Oh, cripes. Jane closed her eyes for a minute. "Brody, remember when I told you I get strong feelings about people."

"Yeah."

"Well, I know that we, you and me, are not to be. I won't give you advice about your relationship with Sadie. Still, I want you to know that whatever you decide, you and I will never happen." Inwardly she sighed. She had fantasized about a night or two with him. Oh yes, she had fantasized. But she knew in her bones, that he was not meant for her.

He rubbed the stubble growing on his chin. "You might change your mind if you spent more time with me. We've never had a chance. I thought maybe we could just have a night or two together."

The door opened, and Gavin MacGregor walked in. A taller and more seasoned version of Brody, he took Jane's breath away. He strode over to her desk and crossed his arms. A storm brewed in his eyes. "You didn't kiss him, did you?"

The deep dulcet tone of his voice raked her senses. Jane laughed. "No, detective. I was just telling him that we will never kiss."

The look of relief on the copper's face hit Jane hard. Hmm, she thought. Something's going on here. The Fates are toying with my life yet again.

Gavin looked at his younger cousin. "Doesn't your shift at the garage start soon? I'll help Jane put her sign up or whatever she needs to do."

The sign. "Dial Witch!" Gavin remembered.

Vixen rolled her eyes.

NINETEEN

"Forget love. Fall in coffee." ~ Anonymous

Cassie rubbed her aching head. Alessandro had argued until the last drop of darkness diminished. She had forgotten how infuriating his stubbornness could be.

Sid raised her chin. "Yah, yah. The vampire's oration is about as elegant as a toad's fart in a swamp, but you must remember he has other skills, Cassie. Other skills."

Cassie rolled her eyes. Thank the heavens, the sun rose, and she had a morning coffee.

"Other skills, Cassie." Sid sent her a triple-X rated memory.

With a smirk, Cassie stirred her brew and wished for inner-peace. She couldn't allow herself the luxury of spending the day fuming over a dead guy.

Well, she could, but she wouldn't. She wanted to get back to the murder.

But her mind went back to Sanjay. Why the hex hadn't he contacted her? It didn't make sense.

She stirred her dark drink and wished for serenity.

Warlocks were secretive by nature, and he was every bit a warlock. Maybe he needed time on his own? But that explanation didn't feel right either.

Hmm. Sanjay's father had been ill

.

No. Something wasn't right. That's all she knew for sure.

"Cassie, you wanted to work on the murder," Sid reminded her.

"Yes. I need to think of someone else."

The two best places to catch up on gossip in town were The Perfect Brew and The Rusty Anchor. It was too early in the day to visit the bar, so she decided to do her sleuthing downstairs. Maybe someone could tell her more about Zabrina's love triangle, or about the mysterious Mr. Mullins who pulled his funding for the art studio.

Sid's whiskers twitched.

"Oh, be quiet," she said to her cat.

"Love is in the air," the familiar said. "That's all I'm saying. Lusty love is in the air."

"Cats," Cassie growled.

When they arrived downstairs, The Brew was in full morning swing. Bright morning sunlight cascaded through the windows giving it a heavenly ambiance. The baristas served an endless line of smiling customers anticipating their morning fix. Cassie sat at her favorite table by the fire and watched the normalcy of daily life in her small-town cafe.

A perfect brew materialized in front of her. She took a sip and sighed. This cup tasted different, more chocolatey than her usual blend, but it hit the spot.

Five nurses in scrubs from the local clinic came and went with their own travel mugs.

A crew from the hydro company sat at a long table in the middle of the room. Eavesdropping on their conversation, Cassie learned that they had been up for hours fixing a power outage at the edge of town where a tree had broken the line. They thought it was lightning, but it might have been magic.

Two teachers from the local elementary school came in talking about the new cut-backs. Having a soft spot for educators, Oscar gave them double-doozies. They headed back out into the stark, winter sunlight.

Twenty minutes passed. No leads. Cassie rubbed her ring finger and wondered about Sanjay. If anyone had asked her if she thought she would fall so hard for a warlock, she would have laughed in their face. But she had fallen. Hard.

They say the Goddess is in the details, and she got that. Maybe love was too.

It wasn't anyone big thing that made her tumble hopelessly in love with him. It was all the little things. The way his voice turned raw when he called her *honey*. The way he brought her a chocolate croissant and coffee on Saturday mornings. The way he made her laugh at life and herself. He always saw the best in her, and he never ever put her down. He never tried to change her like her family had. He never dominated her, like Alessandro had. And she knew, he never would. He simply loved her, truly loved her, and made her feel cherished beyond measure.

Cassie had found her perfect mate, an equal in all ways.

Why the hex didn't he call?

Stormy slid into the seat opposite Cassie and pulled her latest knitting project out of her bag. She was using bright blue wool today. The clicking of the four bamboo needles soothed Cassie's frazzled nerves. It felt as if order to the universe had been restored if only for a moment. A drink appeared in front of the sea witch.

After five peaceful minutes, Stormy spoke. "So, where's the warlock?"

"Family business."

"You don't sound convinced."

Darn her. Stormy had an ear for trouble, just like Cassie's Grandma. "I'm not." She leaned forward. "I understand that family stuff happens. But I don't get why he hasn't contacted me."

Stormy's eyes peered over her reading glasses. "He did this before, did he not?"

"True, he did disappear before, but that was for an initiation ceremony. And it ..." Cassie searched for the right words. "It felt different. If that makes any sense."

"How does it feel different?" Stormy leaned in.

"I knew. I just knew Sanjay was okay. But this time..."

"You're not sure."

Cassie leaned back. "I tried using crystals and Bob, but I can't locate him. I'm still not good enough."

Stormy's mouth scrunched as she looked at her knitting. "You are that good. It sounds like something's wrong, and it sounds to me like you already know that."

"Can I trust my intuition?"

Stormy twirled a needle in the air. "You, my dear, are a talented sorceress. Your senses are talking to you. Listen to them. It's more than intuition." She tugged on her wool, loosening it from the skein resting in her bag. "What are you going to do about it?"

Cassie sensed the wisdom in the older witch's words. She did know something was wrong. "I'm waiting for now. I want to see if he can sort things out for himself. You know how independent he is."

"Sanjay is a rogue warlock in his prime."

"I'm going to focus on Zabrina's murder today. If Sanjay doesn't turn up by dawn tomorrow, I'll go to the Keep and talk with the warriors."

"That's reasonable, as long as you can keep your vampire at arm's length."

"How did you know?" Cassie shook her head. "You know everything that's going on."

"Not everything, but I do know that bloodsuckers are dangerous. The smell of the living-dead hangs on you. You need to be careful. The sexy night-stalker is stalking you."

Cassie sighed. "Yeah, yeah. I can handle Alessandro." She took another sip of her perfect brew. "Since you know so much." She paused. "Can you tell me who killed Zabrina?"

"No, dear, I'm sorry I cannot."

"Do you know anything about a man by the name of Mullins who pulled his funding from Zabrina's studio project?"

"Hmm. Let's see." Stormy calked her head to one side and closed her eyes while her fingers continued to knit. "Yes. Yes. Mullins is from Seattle. He whisks in and out of town, supplying the local stores with cheap touristy items made in China. You know key chains that have a picture of The Keep on them, and calendars that feature photos of the area."

"Do you know what sort of man he is?"

"Mundane, though I thought I got a whiff of an elf scent on him last week. If he isn't part elfin, he might associate with them."

"Did you get the sense that he was evil?"

"Hmph. Cassie dear, you of all witches should know that everyone is capable of evil. Did I get the sense that he leaned that way? No. I can't say I did, but then again, I was eating a salted caramel ice-cream cone. As you know, they are a weakness, and they tend to numb my senses."

Cassie smiled. "Any idea where I can find him?"

"When he's in town, he stays in a room above The Rusty Anchor bar."

Cassie stood and squeezed Stormy's shoulder. "When this is all over, we need to go for an ice-cream cone. My treat."

The older witch gave her a weary smile. "If we both make it through the battle that is to come, then we will feast on ice cream. I'll hold you to that."

A chill ran up Cassie's spine, but she shook it off. It must be the weather, she thought. Winter gets to everyone.

TWENTY

"I begin each day with coffee and the obituaries." ∼ Stormy

Cassie walked to the harbor, hoping the fresh air would clear her mind. It didn't.

A bar had graced the end of the dock for as long as anyone in town could remember. For the last forty years, it had been called The Rusty Anchor and was managed by the Campbell family. Housed in a wooden building with faded paint and adorned by a crooked sign, it looked as if it had washed ashore with the tide.

Inside, the air smelled of beer, charred burgers, and grease. Cassie sat on a stool by the bar and pretended not to stare at the new bartender. Wearing a blue flannel shirt that showed off his broad shoulders, he looked like a guy in Romance movies set in the country. How had she not heard of him? His rolled-up sleeves revealed detailed, dragon tattoos spread over nicely shaped forearms. She tried not to stare.

Why the hex was it, that handsome men appeared everywhere after she fell in love? As the bartender walked towards her, she might have sighed. He was six feet of muscle on a lean frame and had just enough scruff on his square chin to set her hormones humming.

She needed to focus on her mission. What was her purpose? Sid, who sat outside, picked up on her energy and purred.

Cassie bit her bottom lip and recalled her last visit to the bar. The witches in town held a bridal shower here for Belle, who married Oscar. There had been a lot of laughter that night, good laughter, the kind that comes from the belly. Yeah, that was a good memory to dwell on, she thought, as the walking dragon tattoo approached.

He stopped in front of her and leaned forward. "Of all the bars, in all the world, you chose to come into mine." His low, rumbling voice could raise the dead.

Dragon. That synched it. She drank in his scent along with his intoxicating magic. She couldn't be blamed for being attracted to him. He was a dragon!

His full lips hitched on one side, acknowledging her response. He probably made all witches weak.

"Haven't seen you here before," he said. "I would remember you."

"I'm looking for someone."

"I'm available." He chuckled. "Sorry, I couldn't resist the line. I collect cheesy lines."

She smiled back at him. "Mullins. Does that name mean anything to you?" Was she blushing? Possibly. Her hormones wouldn't settle down.

"Last I saw him, he was playing pool over there." The dragon-man pointed towards the back of the old-fashioned saloon. "I hope I'm not going to have any witch trouble. I'm new here."

"Witch trouble?" Cassie said as she climbed down from

the stool with her drink in her trembling hand. "I'm not looking for any kind of trouble, Mr. Dragon."

His eyes flamed blue for an instant, confirming her suspicion. In her bones, she could feel his power.

"My name is Earnest. I am of the Emerald clan."

Cassie nodded. "Your kind are rare. I am honored to make your acquaintance."

"Enchantée," he said.

His scent, a mixture of snow, ice, and sky infused with a magic as old as time, made her head dizzy. "My name is ..."

"Cassie Black. Yes, I know. I know all about you, your aunt, and this town. Your magic drew me here."

Cassie felt her brows rise. "Okay?" she said slowly. Dragons were rarely seen anywhere. They lived in the mountains and preferred their own company.

"I have answered the call of the Warriors, to stand with the magic folk against Erebus."

"Then, I am doubly honored to meet you."

"We cannot let the haven your family has created, be destroyed. Nor can we let darkness prevail." He glanced at the back of the room. "Do you need help with the man named Mullins?"

"I don't think so, but I'll let you know." Cassie checked out the growing crowd.

Mullins stood by the pool table with a cue stick in his hand. He had loosened his striped tie, unbuttoned the top of his white shirt and rolled up his sleeves. In his mouth, he held a cigar firmly between his lips. His salt and pepper hair, heavy on the salt, had been combed over a sizeable bald spot. His face, like his body, was round with fat, and his dark gray eyes looked vacant as if he no longer cared about what he saw.

Two locals, Tim Bradshaw and Luke Gavis, who she

knew from The Brew, played the game with Mullins. They were the town's pool sharks and had a reputation for fleecing newbies. The air around the competition was intense, so she guessed they had started to reel him in.

The geometry of the game intrigued Cassie, but she was not a player. She walked up to Mullins and poked his shoulder. "Excuse me, sir. My name is Cassie Black. Could I have a word?"

Bradshaw and Gavis gave her dagger-stares, but she ignored them.

Mullins took the cigar out of his mouth, swiped it with the back of his hand, and gave Cassie a good once-over look. The kind no woman wants. The way his eyes lurked in particular places made her squirm. "As soon as this game is over, sweetie."

There were worse things to be called than 'sweetie." At this particular moment, Cassie couldn't think of any, and being groped by his eyes made her feel slimy. "Now," she demanded, adding a bit of magic umph to the word.

Bradshaw relented first. "We'll wait," he said and nodded at Cassie.

She smiled at him. Yes, she knew all about him from the witches in town. Ginger had shared all the juicy details, the good, the bad, and the plain weird, during the weekly witch's poker game. All in all, she considered him not a bad guy, but not worthy of a second date.

Gavis punched his friend in the arm. "What the ..."

"Trust me, you don't mess with the ladies at The Brew," Bradshaw said in a low, conspiratorial voice. "Ever."

Smart man, Cassie thought. She stared at Mullins.

"Okay, I'll be back in a five." He followed Cassie to a quiet corner of the bar.

Cassie sat. He grabbed a chair and sat beside her. Ew,

just ew. She invoked a spell, creating an invisible wall between them, shielding her from the stale-beer smell of his breath and any wandering hands.

"I'll get right to the point," she said. "Why did you withdraw your funding for the town's art studio?"

His weary eyes flinched. "Why do you care?"

"Well, I was considering investing myself, and I wanted to find out if there was something bad about the plan I should know about."

"I see." He sucked on his foul cigar and leaned back as if the question required deep concentration. Exhaling slowly, he scrunched his face. "Art just isn't my thing."

Okay. "Did you know Zabrina Zarata well? I understand she was the one who came up with the idea."

"Yeah." Over my shoulders, he surveyed the room as if the answer lay hidden out there somewhere. After a minute, his eyes wandered back. "The proposal didn't make money sense. I have to be honest. I like to support the community. I do. But at the end of the day, I have to make a profit. A man has to eat."

"It must have been hard on Zabrina when you told her you changed your mind."

He sniffed. "I didn't tell Zabrina. But when she found out, she called me up and did a lot of yelling. I think she thought I'd support her because I liked her. I don't have that kind of money."

"Did you know she was murdered two nights ago?"

His face fell. "Hell, no. You can't think I had anything to do with that!"

"Where were you two nights ago?"

"I was at home with my family in Seattle. You can phone my wife." He pulled his business card out of his wallet. "The second number is my home phone line. You can reach her there."

The color in his face had drained. He looked sincerely mortified. "Do the cops know who did it?"

Cassie accepted the business card. "Not yet."

Earnest appeared beside the table. "Can I get you, folks, anything?" His low baritone sounded as smooth as Canadian whiskey.

"No, thanks," I said. "I'm leaving."

Outside, the fresh salt air invigorated her, and she strode towards The Brew. "I didn't care for Mullins, but he was honest."

"That he was," said Sid.

Why did the usually annoyingly-talkative cat have so little to say? "You liked Mullins's cigar smoke." The familiar would have smelled it through Cassie's senses.

"Oh, good goddess, no."

"What is it then? Do you think Mullins killed Zabrina?"

"No."

One word answers! What next? The apocalypse? "What then?"

She purred. "Earnest. He's a lot to take in."

Cassie smiled. "That he is. Do you have another crush? I'll tell Sanjay on you. Or how about Alessandro?"

"A dragon, Cassie." His tail jerked in the air. "A rare dragon has come to our little town. That bothers me in many, many ways."

Cassie stopped laughing. "Me, too, Sid. Me too."

TWENTY-ONE

"Coffee: rocket fuel for the morning impaired." ~
Anonymous

As Cassie looked out her window at the town, she wondered once again about Sanjay. Where the hex was he?

Good grief! He's a bad-boy warlock and perfectly capable of taking care of himself. She swallowed. Why was it so hard to keep believing that he was okay?

The murder. Cassie needed to focus on that. So far, she had three solid suspects: Stardust, Fred Thomas, and Mullins. Through interviewing them, she had learned more about Zabrina than she wanted to know, and none of the suspects felt right.

"Stardust and Kyle have motives, but they also had alibis," said Sid, who jumped on the sofa to stretch out. "If you ask me, the number cruncher is a lover, not a killer. He just doesn't have it in him."

"True and true," said Cassie. "Theoretically, something might have happened that we don't know about that provoked Fred to murder Zabrina in a fit of rage."

"Nah," said Sid stretching her paws.

"Nah," agreed Cassie. "He's just not like that."

"What did you think of Mullins?" asked Sid as she twitched her whiskers.

Cassie laughed. "He's a scumbag through and through. I suspect he offered her money in hopes of getting her into bed and took the offer back when he struck out. I could phone his wife, but I think that would be a waste of my time. I'll give his number to Gavin."

Sid jumped up on Cassie's shoulder.

"Yeah, we're out of suspects," said Cassie.

Sid purred in her ear, a low rumbling sound, to comfort her.

"I could ask Earnest to come with me and get his take on her. Dragons are supposed to be good at interrogations."

Sid purred at the mention of the dragon shifter's name. "The Rusty Anchor does have a reputation for being an excellent source of gossip."

Cassie nodded. "Gavin might have some leads. I could call him. Maybe, he would meet me at the bar?"

"Jane would go with you," said Sid narrowing her eyes.

"Maybe." Jane had been gone all day, getting her stupid store ready. Cassie could use her help.

They stood in silence for a few minutes, and Cassie's mind drifted back to Sanjay. Where the hex was he?

"Get a grip on your broom," grumbled Sid.

Cassie laughed. "Yeah. I guess I sound pathetic. He hasn't been gone that long."

"Not pathetic. Just worried. But worry won't do you, or Sanjay, any good. For the love of all that's holy, do something with your energy." Sid lifted her face. "The old Cassie would wait for Sanjay to turn up, but the new Cassie isn't the kind of witch who waits for a warlock. Get on with your life."

Cassie had lived with Sid for thirty years, and the cat still amazed her. The familiar knew her inside out, and as usual—annoyingly usual—Sid was absolutely right. Cassie couldn't just wait. "I'm going to the Keep."

Built on a cliff high above the harbor, the Keep had been a sanctuary for magic through the centuries. Six months ago, Donovan took command of it and made it the head-quarters for the Warriors, the group of supernaturals who protected the town.

Without a moment's thought, Cassie created a magical portal of scarlet light and stepped through it with Sid. She reappeared in the meeting room of The Warriors.

Donovan, dressed in his warlock battle suit, stood. "You broke through my wards."

Cassie shrugged. "I need to speak to you." It wasn't time to get into a warlock pissing match over territory.

His eyes widened. "I think you know everyone at the table."

Pussy Nip, a petite werecat who wears spandex way too well, stood. She had the annoying habit of purring when-ever Sanjay entered a room. But here, as the leader of the shifters, she appeared to be all business. "Welcome, Cassie," she said.

Hank Henderson, a seven-foot gargoyle dressed in battle fatigues, stood next. "We are at your service, Cassie," he said and bowed.

Zatara of Xanadu, the sorcerer who knew more about arcane spells than anyone else alive, rose slowly. "Madam, it is a pleasure to meet the great-grand-niece of Ophelia."

The power in the room gave Cassie a start, but she had more important things to think about. "Sanjay is missing."

"What do you mean, he's missing?" said Pussy. "You had a lover's quarrel, and he walked out, or demons dragged him away?"

Without a word, Zatara conjured a crystal ball and manipulated it with his hands.

Hank walked to the window and looked towards the city. His wings grew and pulsated with energy.

Donovan stared into Cassie's eyes. "Tell us what you know."

"It's more about what I feel, than what I know. Sanjay's in danger. He's somewhere out there, and he can't communicate with me. Something bad has happened."

Pussy came to her side. "Tell us more."

Zatara spoke. "She's right." The dulcet timbre of his voice shook the room.

They walked over to him and looked in his crystal ball. Cotton-candy clouds rotated around the orb, and in the middle, Peregrine flew, screeching for his master. They had been separated!

Cassie swallowed. "Two days ago, just before Sanjay planned to come here for a meeting, he received a flame text. He turned to me and said, 'My father's ill,' and vanished. At the time, I thought nothing of it. His father has a weak heart. When he didn't text me afterward, I figured he had gotten caught up in the situation. But it's been two days, and I haven't heard from him."

"And you have that awful feeling in the pit of your stomach," added Pussy.

"Exactly."

Hank put a cold, stone arm around her shoulders. "We'll find him," he said.

Donovan asked Zatara, "Can you get a reading on Sanjay's location?"

"Not yet," he replied. "I'll get my team working their crystals. I suggest you contact The Brotherhood."

"Yes," said Donovan. "I will send a flaming text to Sanjay's father right away." He walked over to the windows and chanted a spell beneath his breath. A bright red flame rose in the air between his hands, he worked it with his fingers, chanted another spell, and let it go. It flew out into the wind and disappeared.

"Shall I send our shifters out to look for him?" Pussy asked Donovan.

"Not yet. We need the shifters here. Erebus is about to attack."

Zatara looked up from his crystal ball. "The Dark Lord may have taken Sanjay to distract us and divide our forces. We must consider that possibility."

"Hmm," said Donovan.

Pussy strode over to him and rubbed the leader's arm. He pushed her away. "I need space."

She hissed.

"I am a warlock, Pussy. I need to create a mind-lock with Sanjay. I can't do that when you're all over me."

Pussy turned away and rolled her eyes. "I was trying to be helpful."

The scene would have been funny on any other day, a serious warlock warrior teased by a nymphomaniacal werecat who had the hots for him. But it wasn't funny today. Cassie sighed deeply. "We need Sanjay. You must release forces to look for him." She strode over to Donovan to make her point.

Donovan O'Reilly sank to the floor and crossed his legs. He mumbled an incantation, and the air around him buzzed with energy.

Warlocks! Why can't they explain themselves?

TWENTY-TWO

"As long as there is coffee in the world, how bad could it be." ~ Cassandra Clare, *City of Ashes*

Jane danced in the middle of her store with an audience of one. Gavin, who had finished putting up her sign, "Dial Witch," admired her from the street. His mouth hitched up on one side, exposing his dimple, which made Jane groan inwardly. She crooked her finger and mouthed, "Come in."

Later she would learn all the things that went on in Gavin's mind and heart as he watched her dance that day. But today he simply said, "It's done. Your sign is up. You're in business."

Jane threw her arms around him and hugged him hard.

The cop swallowed, put his hands on her hips, and took a step back. "Just don't kiss me," he said.

She laughed. "Don't worry, I won't kiss you until you're ready." She winked. What the hex was happening? The chemistry between them sizzled.

His cell phone rang. "Excuse me a minute." He walked

to the corner of the store and listened to whatever the caller had to say. His aura flipped out. He glanced at her with a look of horror.

"Gavin?"

He ran for the front door. Over his shoulder, he called, "Lock yourself in. We're under attack."

Like she would do that? He had a lot to learn about her.

Jane followed him onto the sidewalk. He looked up and down the street and then back at her. She lifted her hands and created a safe bubble around them.

He winced. "There's been a report. A pack of supernaturally large wolves is running through the streets, taking down any living thing in their path."

Jane swore.

"My sentiments, exactly. Go back to your store, and .... Lock. Yourself. In."

Jane flipped her red curls over her shoulder. "I can help. I'm a witch, remember. I am your best ally."

But her words were lost in the wind, as he jumped into his truck and reversed onto the road. He leaned out his window. "Lock. Yourself. In."

She put her hands on her hips. "No."

His truck screeched to a full stop, and he hopped out. "Listen, it's no time to play all witchy. Be sensible, you ..."

He didn't finish his sentence. A monster of a wolf leaped through the air, pierced the protective bubble with his claws, and landed on Jane. She screamed as she fell to the pavement.

GAVIN PULLED HIS GUN, but he didn't dare shoot. Jane wrestled with the animal, and they tumbled over and over each other. He didn't want to hit her by mistake. Jane kicked, swore, and scratched. The beast bit into her shoulder, and she shrieked. Desperate, Gavin took aim and shot. The creature cried out. Gavin kicked him off of Jane, and its body ignited in flames.

Blood ran from Jane's shoulder, but her eyes looked angry, not scared. As he helped her to her feet, another hound attacked. He threw his body in front of her this time, and the beast took him to the ground. It sank its teeth into Gavin's neck.

JANE PULLED on her magic to move the wolf. It took a whole minute, but finally, the lupine released Gavin and turned its wild head towards her. The look in its eyes telegraphed its intent. He had been sent to kill her. He left the cop's limp body covered in blood and prepared to launch at her.

Jane was ready. She summoned all her magic and spun it between her hands. When the hound leaped, she shot her power towards him, a lightning bolt of deadly energy. The wolf yelped and fell to the ground. His body caught fire. The smell of burned hair rose in the air.

Gavin lay motionless on the ground. With the help of her magic, she pulled him inside her store. He still had a pulse.

Quickly she strengthened her private wards and her security spells on the store. She grabbed her shawl, and as she wound it tightly around Gavin's neck to help stop the bleeding, she recited a healing incantation. But the flow of blood didn't stop.

She pulled Gavin's radio out and screamed, "Cop down." After she rattled off the details, she used her cell to send a text to Cassie, Oscar, and Donovan. Tears rolled down her face. Gavin didn't have much life left in him.

Vixen stood by her side, meowing quietly.

"Please, don't let him die. Please, please, don't let him die. Please." Jane begged the universe as she cradled him in her arms. "Not Gavin. Please, not Gavin."

TWENTY-THREE

"Coffee makes me user-friendly." ~ The Coffee Queen,
Facebook

Sanjay lay motionless on the floor of his cell. He couldn't
see what was happening in Mystic Keep, but he could feel it
through his connections to people. Darkness rose relent-
lessly like a King tide swallowing everything beneath it.
Chaos would precede the end of life as they knew it. Darkness had come.

And he could do nothing about it.

The people he loved were all at risk. In the distance, he
sensed Peregrine calling to him, but he could make no
contact. Black magic spells surrounded him, stilling his
magic. His warlock senses ached to be released.

The old wooden door of his cell creaked open on rusty
hinges, and the old sorcerer, Brakenfeld, entered. A raven
perched on his left shoulder. "Good day, Sanjay." He
laughed. "At least it's a good day for me."

Sanjay didn't answer.

"Don't look so glum, young warlock. I have a proposition for you."

A proposition? Yesterday the asshole had wanted nothing but pain from him. The deep cuts on his back still bled.

Now he wanted something more? Sanjay sat up and brushed the dirt off his pants. "What now?"

Brakenfeld's face darkened. "I'll get right to it. As you know, I wanted to keep you for myself. I wanted to feel your pain, every little bit of it until you died."

Sanjay waited.

"But," said his nemesis. "I have been given an offer I can't refuse."

"You're going to sell me?"

"Yes. How astute of you. When news got out that I own you, so to speak, several interested parties started a bidding war."

"The Brotherhood?" For an instant, Sanjay felt hope.

"Oh, please. Like I would cooperate with them. They don't have that kind of money anyway. No. No. No. Not *The* Warlock Brotherhood." He waved his hand.

"Who then?"

"Two powerful, dark sorcerers, adept practitioner of black magic. They want your body and soul. Each offered me a lot of money." As Brackenfeld paced the floor in front of Sanjay, his long dark shadow cast a chill in the room. "Who knew the likes of you would be valuable?" The old warlock sighed dramatically. "And as much as I enjoy your pain, I enjoy money more."

Sanjay didn't know whether to be happy or sad. Maybe a new captor might be easier to escape from or coerce.

Rubbing his chin, Brakenfeld said, "I suspect they want

to tear you apart, study the insides of a royal warlock, you know. Dissect you like a bug. I like that idea. Hmm."

The older man turned on his heel and continued pacing. "Or, perhaps, they'll use your DNA to clone an army." He sighed. "I'm not really sure what they want you for. Nor do I care, really."

Sanjay growled.

The older warlock flapped his arms and grinned like a boy who had just caught his first fish. "I neither know nor care why they want you. All that really matters is the money. You're worth a surprising amount of gold, more than I could spend in a lifetime. It will buy me security, luxury, and a harem of willing women." He kicked Sanjay's foot and continued his walk.

The kick hurt, but Sanjay refused to show it.

"My dilemma," continued Brakenfeld, "is that if I intend to sell you, I have to forgo torturing you. They want you in good health, you see. And I ..." He sighed like a drama queen in a teenage sit-com. "I was so looking forward to torturing you." He grunted. "So, I can sell you and make money, or I can keep you and relish in my revenge plans." He grimaced.

"It sucks to be you," Sanjay said in a flat voice. "So many choices and so little time." He stared at the older magi with all the hatred he felt. While the prison muted his magic, it didn't touch his hatred.

Brakenfeld flinched. "Yes. Yes. It does suck to be me. But ..." He leered at Sanjay. "Either way, I get my revenge."

Sanjay rolled his eyes. "You mentioned a proposition."

"Yes, well." Brakenfeld crouched to look Sanjay in the eyes. "The sorcerer who offered the most money stipulated that you must not only be unharmed, but also willing ..."

Sanjay stood. "And what would make me willing to be sold?"

The older warlock rose. "In return for your willingness, I would promise to never hurt Cassie or your unborn child."

Unborn child? What the hell?

Brakenfeld's evil smile froze on his face. "You didn't know, did you?"

TWENTY-FOUR

"I can't stop drinking the coffee. I stop drinking the coffee, I stop doing the standing, and the walking, and the words-putting-into-sentences doing." ~ Lorelai Gilmore, Gilmore Girls

Merlina Black, Cassie's oldest sister, could feel her sisters' pain. She usually blocked it out. Having five eccentric, witchy sisters meant she lived within a soap opera of emotions. At least one of them was unhappy at any given moment. She loved her sisters dearly, but she had learned to put up boundaries to protect herself. The golden rule of being a witch-empath was to take of yourself first so that you remained capable of helping others.

When an overwhelming sense of emotional distress came from Cassie, and Jane burst through all her wards, Merlina fell to the ground. The feelings washed over her, constricting her chest and leaving her gasping for breath. Never had she felt so distressed. Her sisters in that small town with the funny name needed her.

Within a minute, she materialized beside Jane, because

she was usually in the most trouble. Jane sat on the floor of a shop cradling a man covered in blood. Tears streamed down her face. "No. Not Gavin," she wailed.

Merlina was the most powerful of all the witches in her family and, for that matter, in her coven. She flicked her hands upwards and froze the moment. Jane, unaffected because of her own magic, turned to look at her.

"What happened?" Merlina demanded as she bent down to feel for the stranger's neck pulse.

"I. I. I think they killed him." Her voice hitched. "He saved me."

His pulse rang through Merlina's senses, slow and steady. "He's alive," she said. "Barely. But he is alive."

"I've called an ambulance and others," said Jane, stroking Gavin's hair. "He shouldn't have been here. He shouldn't have protected me."

Merlina looked to the heavens for support. "Jane, get a hold of yourself. My frozen-spell will only last a couple minutes. I need the Cauldron's short notes on what the hex is going on here."

Jane took a deeper breath. "Darkness has come to our little town." She took another breath. "Erebus, the Lord of Darkness, sent a pack of demon-wolves through the streets. Gavin is a cop, and he shot several. I vanquished a few. But there were so many. One leaped in the air, broke through my protection spells, and landed on me. Gavin killed it. Then another attacked, and Gavin put himself in front of me. He was bit protecting me."

Merlina could feel her brows rising. What the hex had her sisters been up to? Maybe they had something funny going on in the local water supply. Whatever. The fact remained the mundane man was close to death. There wasn't time to unpack the details. His life force was leaving this plane.

Pulling magic from every cell of her body, she pushed it through her hands, creating a stream of warm energy, and covered his body with it, as if it were a blanket.

Jane added her magic to the spell and looked to her sister for direction.

OUTSIDE, the world had stilled because of Merlina's spell. The witches focused on keeping Gavin's heart beating.

A golden swirl of magic appeared beside them, and Donovan O'Reilly appeared with his sword drawn.

O'REILLY HAD BEEN busy with a Warriors meeting at The Keep when he got the emergency cry for help from Jane. In the next instant, one of the clairvoyants declared that wolves were running through the town hunting and attacking supernatural beings. Fearing the worst, he answered Jane's distress call.

Jane, he knew through Cassie, but the other witch, he had never seen. Her magic vibrated through the room as she chanted a healing spell over Gavin. This was a witch of remarkable power.

Who the hex was she? He blinked. She had to be new. Her face turned to look at him for a brief second, and in that instant, he knew all he needed to know about her.

The woman was a more mature version of Cassie and Jane. She had to be their sister. Same heart-shaped face. Same brow. Same full, sensuous mouth. Her thick, dark brown hair had been woven into a thick braid revealing a wise face.

Donovan sheathed his sword, threw back his cape, and raised his magic. As he added his energy to that of the witches, a humming sound spread around them. Gavin's body rose three inches above the ground, and his heartbeat strengthened.

Merlina's freezing spell dissipated.

Sirens wailing in the distance grew closer.

Minutes later, the first responders ran into the room, with the police behind them. Gently the witches and warlock let Gavin's body fall to the floor, and the medics took over.

Merlina pulled Jane into her arms and held her close. Donovan put his hand on Jane's back and said nothing. They hadn't been able to stop Gavin's wound from bleeding, and the chances of living were slim.

CASSIE MATERIALIZED and took in the scene. Donovan put an arm around her. "We did our best."

This couldn't be happening, Cassie thought. This just couldn't be happening.

Jane pulled away from Merlina and shook her head. "It's my fault," she said.

Cassie took one look at Merlina and nodded. "You came to help us. Thank you."

Merlina closed her eyes, like a cat. "Actually, I came to see what the hex you were up to in a town named after a lighthouse. What's this about Erebus and demon-wolves?"

"If he dies, it's because of me," said Jane through trembling lips.

"Nonsense," said Merlina. "If he dies, it is the will of the universe. We did everything we could to save him."

"But he didn't have to ..."

"Jane," said Donovan, "Gavin is a warrior. He always knew he might die fighting evil. It was a risk he willingly took to protect others."

"Don't talk about him in the past tense," Jane said.

Merlina shushed her. "Keep breathing, Jane. He isn't dead."

"Demon- wolves?" said Cassie.

Merlina sighed. "I didn't see them, but I smelled the rank odor of a rogue werewolf on his skin."

Donovan nodded. "As did I."

"It's all my fault," murmured Jane, almost inaudibly.

TWENTY-FIVE

"Stressed, blessed, and coffee obsessed." ~ Anonymous, Facebook

Cassie watched in horror as two medics wheeled Gavin into the ambulance. The head guy closed the door, and looked at the three witches. "I thought I'd seen everything! But a hovering cop is a first."

As the vehicle pulled away with the siren blaring, the sisters stood silently holding hands. Donovan turned towards them and bowed. "I must return to The Keep. The warriors are waiting."

"Thank you for your help," Cassie said.

O'Reilly pushed his hands together in prayer and bowed. "I'll see you later. Stay safe." With a snap of his fingers he created a golden vortex of energy and stepped into it.

"Okay then," said Merlina. "You witches have some explaining to do. What the hex is a *keep*? Who are the warriors? And where did the hell hounds come from?" She paused for a breath. "And tell me about *that warlock?*" She pointed towards the spot Donovan had vanished from.

Always bossy, thought Cassie, who pasted a smile on her face, and tried to count to ten. She stopped at three. Who was she kidding? Merlina was the, 'She who must be obeyed,' witch in the family, and there was no point trying to push her off her princess throne. Exhaling slowly, she nodded in acceptance. "Okay, Merlina, we have a lot to fill you in on." Where to start? "Perhaps you'd like a cup of coffee."

"Coffee? Hex, no, I want answers."

"It all starts with the coffee," said Jane brushing tears from her face. "Trust me, our brew will help you understand."

BACK AT THE PERFECT BREW, the witches took seats around Cassie's favorite table near the fire. Cassie, motioned towards a chair, for Merlina.

"Wait. Don't we have to order at the bar?"

"No," said Cassie. "I inherited this coffee house from our wild great-aunt Ophelia." She had told her family about this in emails. Obviously Merlina had been too busy to read the details, and if she were honest with herself, she had left the juicier ones out.

Merlina scrunched-up her face. "The one who danced on table tops? And wore sequins?"

"Yes, that one. Along with this business and the building that houses it, I inherited the responsibility of protecting the portal beneath it."

The Brew's lights flickered, and Cassie smiled.

"I see," said Merlina, but Cassie wondered about that.

"And," Cassie continued, "I inherited power."

"You already had that power," said Jane quietly. "You just didn't know you had it. It matured when Ophelia passed."

Three perfect brews materialized in front of the witch sisters in mugs with their names on them. Merlina's brows rose. "Oh, this isn't a normal coffee-house."

Now she's getting it. "No, and that's not a normal coffee." Cassie said as she waved her thanks to Oscar who stood behind the coffee bar.

Merlina's eyes followed the interaction. "Are all the men in Mystic Keep devastatingly sexy, and talented in the ways of magic?"

"Not all," said Cassie, wanting to get on with her explanation.

"What happened to Sanjay?" asked Jane.

Cassie took a sharp breath.

Merlina leaned in. "Okay, so who's Sanjay?"

"What? You didn't tell her about Sanjay?" said Jane.

"I couldn't tell her about Sanjay. The whole family would find out and I just wasn't ready for all of that, and besides, we've been too busy."

"Too busy, eh?" Merlina's eyes narrowed. "I definitely want to know more about Sanjay."

"Basically, he's the bloodsucker's replacement, only much, much better," said Jane.

Cassie glared at her.

"What?" said Jane. "It's the truth." She took a sip of her brew and sighed. "Okay, maybe I was a bit harsh. The only thing Sanjay and Alessandro have in common is that they both love Cassie."

"Oh," said Merlina, who took a sip of her drink and sighed. "So, Cassie's finally off dead men."

Jane grinned. "I'm not sure about that. The bloodsucker's upstairs at the moment." Jane angled her head. "But getting back to Sanjay. He's six feet of drool-worthy, alpha-rogue warlock with royal blood. When he enters a room, everyone stops talking." Jane nodded her head. "But as tough as he appears, he's got a big heart. He's the kind of man who's always there for his friends and enjoys helping people. And ..."

Merlina put up her hand and stared at Cassie. "Wait. Why aren't you saying anything."

Cassie could put a strong face on for most of the world, but not for Merlina. She bit her lip. "Sanjay's missing, and I don't have a good feeling about it."

"Drink your coffee," said Merlina. "You'll feel better." She turned to Jane, "Tell me more. Who are the warriors?"

"Let me start here," said Jane. "Ophelia created this coffee house, The Perfect Brew, as a sanctuary for all supernatural beings. Its power draws our kind, to the town and now the magic folk outnumber the mundanes. To keep the peace a select group of supernatural warriors were chosen as our protectors. Kind of like our own police. They formed a posse a few months ago when we had trouble, which I'll tell you about some other time."

"And Donovan is a warrior" Merlina said.

"He is their leader." Jane and Cassie spoke at once.

"He oversees three teams: shifters, wizards, and others," explained Cassie, who didn't want to remain silent when most of the story really was about her.

Merlina took another sip of her brew. "Hmm."

Cassie enjoyed the momentary silence as her sister digested the information. It wouldn't take her long.

"The hell hounds?" asked Merlina after a minute.

Jane trembled. "Gavin was helping me put up a sign for my new business." She watched Merlina's eyes grow large.

"I'll tell you about that later. It doesn't matter now. He got a call on his cell phone, and rushed out the door. I followed him out. Thirty enormous wolves ran down the center of the road. People scrambled for shelter and locked their doors. Gavin started shooting. I quickly threw up a bubble of protection over us, but it didn't hold. A large white wolf launched into the air towards me and pulled me to the ground. Gavin killed him. Another appeared and he shielded me with his body." Jane closed her eyes. "You know the rest."

"I see." Merlina put her hand over Jane's. "Where did the animals come from?"

"Remember, I mentioned a portal," said Cassie. "It lies beneath this café." She took a gulp of coffee, but she really needed a gallon to explain this one. "It's one of *the thirteen* on earth that connects with other dimensions. Sanjay and I are its guardians."

"And the hounds came from the portal?" Merlina's eyes widened.

"Not exactly," said Cassie. "Around the time Ophelia died, the wards on the portal door were weakened by her absence and the Lord of Darkness, Erebus, came through."

Merlina's eyes narrowed. "That was a while ago. Why is he attacking now?"

"He is responsible for Ophelia's death and he's tried to kill me twice. Six months ago, we fought back."

"But he's been lurking and growing in power. I can feel his presence," said Jane. "All the supernaturals could."

"What does he want?" asked Merlina.

"Power," said Cassie.

"He's already the king of evil. We all know he picks on people's weaknesses and seduces their souls. What more could he possibly want?"

Cassie looked at Merlina.

"Oh! He wants to dominate our world. He wants it all."

Cassie's phone buzzed. "It's a text from Donavan. He wants us to join him at the Keep. But I have to talk with the staff first. They're all kitchen witches and you know how sensitive they can be. Jane, fill Merlina in on anything else you think is important."

TWENTY-SIX

"I'd rather take coffee than compliments just now." ~
Louisa May Alcott, *Little Women*

Twenty minutes later, the three witches materialized outside The Keep. Merlina shivered as she looked up at the tall, stone structure, perching on the edge of a cliff high above the harbor. Jane drew her jacket closer around her body and groaned. She had never liked the place.

Cassie shrugged. "They named this pile of stones the Keep, because it resembles the towers built in Europe during the middle ages, which were used as safe houses. You know, the place they hid in when an enemy stormed their castle."

Cassie walked up to it and put her hand on its side feeling for its sentient pulse. "Our Keep has a storied past and lingering old magic that is simply delicious." She turned and grinned at Merlina. "Donovan made it the meeting place for the warriors. It's his protection wards you feel around it. Only those invited may enter.

Donavan appeared in front of them, as if he heard his

name. His Irish blue eyes took them in with a glance. "Witches, this way," he said.

They climbed a wooden staircase to the second floor, and followed the warlock into the meeting room. Winter sunlight flowed through a bank of five long windows. Water seeped from the stone walls riddled with moss. Magic spells, swirled around them, beckoning them in, but warning them to not stay too long. The damp air smelled of white sorcery.

The three Warrior leaders stood upon their arrival. Cassie quickly introduced Merlina to Hank Henderson the gargoyle, Pussy Nip the shifter, and Zatara the sorcerer. She noticed her sister's smile tightened on one side at the mention of the werecat's name.

"Have you found Sanjay?" Cassie asked.

Donovan motioned for them to take seats at their table, which was cluttered with crystal balls, pots of magic potions, and collections of herbs. Each had a mug of perfect brew in front of them courtesy, no doubt, of Oscar.

As soon as they sat, Donovan waved his hands in the air and a holographic map appeared on the wall. The first image was that of earth. The warlock closed his eyes and moved the fingers on his right hand in a precise way to conjure an image of six other realms "These," he said, "are the closest dimensions. Cloudy images of faraway lands, exotic and remote in every sense appeared. As soon as we exhausted our search of earth we began looking towards them. But our quest is temporarily on hold, as we are under attack."

He turned to the others. "I have called us all together for an update on our battle with the wolves," said Donovan. "Henderson?"

Hank Henderson, the gargoyle stood, and nodded at the

witches. "My team has been chasing the pack of wolves running through town. We killed thirteen so far, and are doing a second sweep as I speak."

Cassie blinked. There's nothing pretty about war.

As Hank sat down Pussy stood and smiled at the witches. "The shifters have been following on the heels of Hank's crew. We caught five more. Our werewolves determined the attackers are hybrid creatures, part cyborg and part demon." She sat.

Cassie shuddered. Cyborg-demons. "Trust the Lord of Darkness to be a techie," she muttered.

"Good work," said Donovan. "Thank your teams for me. They are keeping us safe." He walked over to the bank of windows. "Hank, we need more warriors working the perimeter of town. Pussy ..."

"The shifters will handle the canopy," she said.

Zatara stood and hit his staff on the stone floor. Everyone turned his way and waited. "Have we any back-up?" he said.

"Yes," said Donovan. "The Warlock Brotherhood is sending a team of nine fighters to assist in protecting the portal and Mystic Keep. They promised to send more within the week. Their Intelligence network is working their magic looking for Sanjay. There are rumors that dark sorcerers are also looking."

"And I see we are gaining witches in our fold," Zatara said.

Donovan smiled. "Yes, and we welcome them."

"I could ask the rest of the family to come," said Jane.

"No. Goodness, no," said Merlina, before Cassie had a chance to speak. "There's enough of us here. You know we just get in each other's way."

The crystal ball sitting directly in front of Zatara, which

had been running long lists of numbers, turned bright red and made a thrumming sound. Everyone stared at it.

Zatara placed his hands above the orb, closed his eyes, and chanted in whispers. Cassie couldn't make out his words, but her heart jumped into her throat in anticipation. He chanted more and more and finally the red haze inside the crystal dissipated and a clear image appeared.

"Sanjay, at last," the old sorcerer said.

Cassie swallowed. She could see Sanjay sitting on a dirt floor, shackled to a stone wall. It looked like an old dungeon. Cuts and bruises covered his swollen face, but his lips pulled into a slow smile. Had he sensed the sorcerer's white magic probing the room? Cassie hoped he did.

"Can you reach him?" Cassie said.

"Where is he?" asked Donovan.

"Zatara raised his hands. As he chanted a white flame appeared between them. He shaped it over and over, and then thrust it towards the image of Sanjay. Behind him on the stone wall of his cell a message appeared. "We are coming."

The words disappeared and Zatara collapsed. Hank caught his body and eased it into the chair. The image of Sanjay smiling widely now, remained.

It took Zatara ten minutes to recover. In the meantime, Hank and Pussy left to attend to the wolves. Cassie paced the floor of the meeting room. Jane phoned the hospital for an update on Gavin. Merlina watched.

Zatara's eyes opened. "I know where to find Sanjay."

TWENTY-SEVEN

"Coffee, the favorite drink of the civilized world." ∼
Thomas Jefferson

Zatara determined a precise location for Sanjay in a tiny dimension that lay hidden between two larger ones. Donovan looked pleased with the news. "I'll inform The Brotherhood and we'll plan an extraction," he said.

"I want to go," said Cassie.

"No," said Donovan.

"But ..."

"No," said Donovan, in a voice that didn't invite discussion. The darn warlock could explain himself well with one word.

Cassie bit her lip. "I could help you."

"Perhaps, but Sanjay would never forgive me, if I put you in harm's way. You must stay here and wait."

Cassie grumbled. "I'm not good at waiting."

"I'll keep you updated." He put a hand on her shoulder. Warmth and compassion flowed through it. "You know we can attack the enemy faster without you."

She wished that wasn't true. But it was. The warlocks were trained to fight in teams. The men selected for the mission would be skilled in warfare and magic, they were the supernatural equivalent of a Navy Seal team.

"Can't I do something?" she said.

"Wait," he said. His Irish-blue eyes nailed her to the wall.

"Okay. Okay," she said, as she slowly backed out of the room.

He folded his arms and the right edge of his mouth quirked-up. It was never a good idea to turn your back on an agitated warlock.

Cassie found herself outside staring up at the stormy sky, wishing she could be more like Pussy Nip, not just because of the weretiger's ability to look good in spandex, but because she was useful in battle.

Sid jumped onto Cassie's shoulder. The cat made no wise crack. No platitude. She said nothing, which was a first for Sid. With a quiet purr she soaked Cassie with compassion and warmth. Cassie took a deep breath and looked at her sisters who walked up to her. "Well we might as well go back to The Brew."

THE QUIETNESS of the town gave Cassie the shivers. The main street, the very heart of their village, was empty. Absolutely empty. People hid in their homes, locked their doors, and closed their shutters. "I imagine the rumor mill is going crazy online," she said.

Jane raised her head from her cell phone. "It's bad."

"How bad?" said Merlina.

"Real bad. Some say the wolves are a political stunt. Others say they came from the labs at the university where they do experiments mixing human and animal genes." She tsked. "But that's not the worst."

Oh hex! "Just tell us," said Cassie. How much worse could this day get?

"Some say they knew this was coming, because strange things keep happening in town."

"Well, strange things do happen in this town," conceded Cassie.

"Wait for it. Witches, they say, cause all the trouble." She grumbled. "Witches."

"Oh, fudge," said Cassie.

"And get this. They have a new hashtag, #burnthe-witches.

Burn. The. Witches! Holy, mother-witcher of magic, could this really be happening? Cassie and Merlina stared over Jane's shoulder at the last community post. It read, "Burn the witches. Burn them all." Signed Concerned Citizen, and tagged #burnthewitches.

"Nice town," Merlina said, in a flat voice.

"It is ... was ... a nice town." Cassie's gut burned as if a thousand cauldrons boiled demon entrails inside her. "Who am I kidding? Rumors about strange happenings in town started before I got here. Great-Aunt Ophelia never learned to fly her broom under the radar, and her friends who followed her here have similar self-monitoring issues."

"I don't have time for this," said Jane. "I'm going to see Gavin." She vanished.

Merlina sighed. "Now I'm totally confused. Jane told me the cop was one of your paramours enraptured by your charm. Something about a kiss ..."

Cassie grunted. "I can't deal with *that* now. I need to focus."

"Men, you mean?" Merlina laughed. "Honey, you never

were good at dealing with them. That's why you chose a dead one for so long."

Cassie glared at her.

"Like I've told you before," Merlina continued, "Men are not just a little bit different from us, they fart in a whole different universe. You know the saying, 'men are from mars.' Well I say men are from ..."

Cassie glared at her sister. "Are you done?"

Merlina gave her a satisfied smile. "Depends. Do you want me to tell you what I think of your warlock?"

"Please, don't." Cassie's words hissed through her clenched jaw. "We have more important issues to deal with." She opened the door of the coffee shop and entered.

As Merlina followed her in, she pulled her cellphone out and tapped on the keys.

What was the bossy witch up to? Should Cassie worry? She stopped and folded her arms. "What are you doing?" she asked.

Merlina tapped a bit more and then turned her screen so that Cassie could read it. Cassie laughed. The post read, "Dear Concerned Citizen, Be careful. Be very careful. It's not easy to catch a witch." She signed it, The Big Bad Witch, and added the hashtag #becarefulwhosbroomyoutouch.

Cassie couldn't stop laughing. Cyber-warfare, witch style. She rubbed at the tears in her eyes. "You know this could make things worse."

"Yeah. Social Media is full of slime balls. Sometimes you have to out-slime them. And you, little sister, need to relax. An exhausted witch is useless."

"You want me to do a crossword puzzle?" That was one of Merlina's favored hobbies.

"No, it seems murder is more up your alley. Let's go find your killer. I understand you're looking for one."

Cassie blinked. Merlina had a point. "There's nothing I can do about Sanjay right now. Jane will take are of Gavin. As much as I hate to admit it, you're right. I could spend more time looking for Zabrina's murderer." She bit her lip. "And you with your logical mind and fresh eyes are the perfect person to help me."

"Good. So, fill me in. Who are your suspects?"

They sat at Cassie's table and drank more brew, which Oscar kept topped. The coffee shop was only half-full, which was unusual for this time of day. A few of their kind sat around tables chatting quietly, but no mundanes were in the crowd. Would this be the way of the future? Their new-normal? Cassie hoped not, but for now she had bigger hexes to fry.

It took ten minutes for Cassie to tell Merlina everything she knew about Zabrina's murder, and the suspects she had interviewed. Going over the details, made her wonder about other suspects. Who else could it be? "You know, I think I'm missing something. I need to talk to Gavin."

"The cop you kissed. Okay, let's go," said Merlina.

JANE LET them in to Gavin's hospital room. "He's doing well, but I think we need to move him."

Cassie walked up to his bed. Gavin's eyes looked cloudy. His arm was attached to an IV apparatus. "Cassie," he said in his low rumbling voice.

"Hi, Gav. I just wanted to make sure the best cop in town was doing okay." She winced at the cheesiness of her own words, as she squeezed his hand.

His boyish grin spread slowly. "Just dandy. Is this

another sister?" He looked at Merlina. "I'm not sure I can handle another."

"Yeah, I'm their big sister." Merlina nodded. "Thanks for saving Jane. Our family owes you."

He shrugged, and muttered, "Just doing my job." But the way he looked at Jane was anything but professional.

A warm fuzzy feeling brewed in Cassie's heart for her younger sister. When had this romance started? Hadn't Jane been crazy about his cousin last week?

"Ouch," Cassie said as Merlina elbowed her.

"Cassie has some questions for you," Merlina said.

Gavin looked at her. "Okay."

"I'm hunting for Zabrina's murderer, looking for the MMO. Means, motive and opportunity. Right?"

Gavin rolled his eyes. "You watch way too much TV. You really should leave murder investigations to the professionals."

To hex with this. Another man telling her to do nothing. Urgh. "Yeah, well, maybe. But the best professional I know in town is laid-up in the hospital. So, cut me some slack. I've discovered Zabrina's love triangle, which provides juicy motives for two people."

"Stardust and Kylo were both seen at the club during the time of the murder," said Gavin, flatly. "Half the town supports their alibi."

Cassie nodded. "I talked with Fred Thomas her accountant friend. He loved her and I don't think he would hurt her in any way."

Gavin said nothing.

"I don't think he's a killing type," she added.

Gavin smirked. He didn't say it, but she knew what he was thinking. Even the gentlest of people can commit a murder given enough provocation.

"I also talked with Mullins, the man who pulled her studio financing. In short, I don't think he did it either. Now what do I do? I'm stumped."

"When you run out of suspects, you start at the beginning again. Ask yourself if you missed anything. Go over the evidence you have. If no other suspects appear, you re-interview the first ones. But Cassie, you shouldn't ..."

"Be interviewing murder suspects," Extra Hot said in a low cop voice. It creeped Cassie out, how quietly the big man entered the room. No one noticed him until he spoke. How much had he heard?

Merlina's brow rose, as she took in the big policeman glaring at her sister, but she said nothing.

"Charles, good to see you," said Gavin. Then he looked at Cassie. "Constable Charles has taken over the investigation."

The man who loved his coffee hot looked at her. His dark brown eyes turned rock hard. "And you won't get around me with your feminine charms, or any other charms."

"Unless she kisses you," muttered Merlina, just loud enough for her sisters to hear. They smiled in unison.

Extra-Hot grumbled. "It's the first time I've been a lead on a murder investigation and no amateur sleuth is getting in my way."

Since when did he get so bossy? Thought Cassie, who, finding herself at a loss for words, stuck her tongue out at him.

TWENTY-EIGHT

"No matter what historians claimed, BC really stood for
'Before Coffee.' " ~Cheriese Sinclair, *Maser of the
Mountain*

The sister witches convened outside Gavin's hospital room.

Jane spoke first. "I'm staying here to protect Gavin. I
don't like the look of his eyes. They're pumping so many
chemicals into his body I can't tell if he's reacting to them,
or something else. Something supernatural." She didn't
have to say what reaction she was really worried about.
They all knew the effects of being bit by a hybrid, demon
wolf were unknown. "I've called Mom," Jane continued. "to
send one of our own doctors to check him out."

"Let's hope she sends Zen," said Merlina.

Cassie nodded as she rubbed the spot between her eyes,
where a killer headache had popped up. It felt like a sledge-
hammer from hell. "That's a good idea," she said.

Merlina looked at one sister and then the other. "I'm
going to make sure Cassie gets some rest. I'll stay with her at
the apartment."

Merlina swooshed her right arm theatrically in a large circle, creating a portal lit with orange flames. It had a sweet, citrus smell that reminded them all of their Grandmother's orange and cranberry scones, and along with them the safety and security of home. Cassie stepped into it and landed in her apartment. Within minutes, she lay in her bed, tucked under a soft quilt with Sid, purring at her side.

But sleep eluded her. Deep in her gut, a gnawing feeling that she should know who killed Zabrina ate away at her. She felt their identity lay just beyond her grasp. If she spent a little bit more time on the case, maybe all the pieces of the puzzle would fall into place. If she only reached a little further into her senses, she would figure it out. She went over the details of the murder, every suspect's interview, Gavin's comments, and everything she knew about that night. Over and over again, she reviewed the case. But to no avail.

Merlina, with a stern looking face, entered Cassie's bedroom. "You're impossible. You always were a lousy patient." She handed Cassie a cup of sleepy tea, a family favorite potion for restless nights, and stood by Cassie's side as she drank it.

Finally, the weight of the world dissolved and minutes later Cassie slid into a deep sleep. Only to dream ...

CASSIE WANDERED through a field of wildflowers dominated by orange poppies, yellow rattle and white clover. Their beauty was beyond description. Their fragrance, rich and complex, was intoxicating. It felt like a meadow in heaven. As she settled into the bliss of the moment, a unicorn trotted up to her side.

Okay, wait. Wait one hexing moment. A unicorn? It was

already unbelievable that she would find herself in a landscape of beauty beyond measure. Add in a unicorn, and it spelled trouble. Woah. Unicorn-woah. This was no ordinary dream.

Cassie's witch senses prickled. Beneath the sweet smell of the flowers, hid the nasty stench of evil.

The unicorn dropped to her knees. Should Cassie mount her? A unicorn! Cassie had never met such a magical beast before, even in her dreams. The temptation was great, but she knew such an adventure would not be without peril. Would the unicorn help her through the danger? Or, was the unicorn the danger?

Why the hex, did her supernatural life not come with instructions. This page should read: When you meet a unicorn in your dreams. Or, how about, When the flowers smell too sweet.

Hashtag: Burnthewitches. Why was her world turning upside-down? Why her? Why couldn't she have a perfect life like other good witches, one with a white picket-fence to lean her broom on?

Oh, to hex with it. Cassie mounted the unicorn and held tightly to her mane as she trotted along the dirt path, through the meadow, to a forest.

Oh, no, thought Cassie. She had read all the classic fairy tales. One should never trust the big, dark forest on the edge. There lay trouble.

Her unicorn, who made no attempt to communicate with her, began to gallop, and within seconds Cassie found herself flying through a forest of tall, conifer trees, filled with dark shadows, and crows. Lots and lots of crows. Too many to be believed. They cawed and swooped down at her head as if she were invading their territory.

Maybe she was.

The unicorn picked up speed. Light appeared at the end of the path and for one, glorious second, she hoped the dark feeling of the forest would be over. They were almost there, almost to the light. Hope filled her heart.

But the dream was not over.

As they leaped into the sunlight, Cassie landed in front of a tall, dark castle. She and the unicorn stood alone on a stone path. Her throat thickened.

What the hex was a dreary, god-forsaken, castle of doom doing in the middle of her wildflower and unicorn dream? Cassie shook her head.

The unicorn lowered herself to the ground, and Cassie slid to her feet. She reached out to touch the magical beast, but she ascended into the sky. The batting of her wings made a loud whooshing sound, as she gained altitude and neared the castle. When she reached the top her image exploded into a ball of shimmering light, and as the light faded, she transformed into a gargoyle, and settled on the side of the dark, stone castle.

Great, thought Cassie, just hunky-dory, great.

The drawbridge, because of course her dark castle would have a drawbridge, clunked down at her feet. Dirt rose from the ground. She peered along the entranceway.

"Nope. I'm not going there," she said out loud. It was her dream after all. Shouldn't she have some control?

"Come to me," said a low male voice. "Come to me, Cassiopeia Black."

Cassie couldn't see anyone, but the voice definitely came from inside the castle.

"No," she said.

The sound of a cat screeching in pain, followed.

"Sid?" she called out. "Sid?" She had only heard her

familiar make such a sound once before when she had been beaten to the edge of her life.

"Come to me," the voice repeated. "Or your beloved cat dies."

It was just a dream, she told herself, just a bad dream, a really, really bad dream. "No," she repeated. "You cannot have me."

"Oh, I will have you. It's just a matter of time, my dear."

Sid spoke in her mind. "I'm doomed either way. Do not go to him, Cassie. Do. Not. Go to him."

How could she not? Sid had saved her life. It was her turn to save hers. "If. If I come to you, will you let my familiar go?"

Silence.

"Please, please, let Sid free. She has done nothing wrong." Cassie fell to her knees pleading.

Sid's howls stopped.

"The cat means nothing to me," said the voice. "But you mean everything."

"Tell me what I can do for you, and I will do it, in exchange for Sid's freedom." What was she thinking. No one won when they bartered with the devil. Why did she think she had a chance?

"Come to me."

Cassie swallowed hard as she watched herself in her dream. The moment of choice had come. There would be no turning back. "Erebus?" she called.

"Yes. It is me, my child."

"I cannot help you. I am a white witch."

He chuckled. "I can fix that. Come to me. I will adopt you, and you will become more powerful." His voice thundered in the dreamscape and the sky turned dark and menacing. "I cannot wait forever." Lightning lit the sky and the sound of thunder pounded.

"Erebus?"

"Sid will not survive long."

"What if I did just one thing for you. What if I let you freely roam in a space on earth."

"No!" Thunder and lightning ripped around her. Rain poured down. "Do not deny me. No one denies me, in the end."

Cassie got to her feet and brushed the dirt from her nightgown. Not that she should care what she looked like when she gave herself to the Lord of all Darkness. She stepped forward. The ground felt solid beneath her feet, but her heart trembled. If she gave in, the portal would be unprotected and all manner of darkness would seep into the world. If she didn't give in, Sid would lose her life. Why could there not be a third option.

There had to be a third option.

At the end of the drawbridge, she came to an enormous, arched doorway, which lay open. She walked through it into a courtyard filled with Gollum-like creatures staring at her through bug eyes. The air stank of death and decay.

As she proceeded to the inner door, the creatures gathered behind her, forming a procession, as if they performed a dark wedding, or funeral procession. Funeral more likely, she thought. My soul's funeral.

The door opened and inside lay darkness. Solid darkness. Darker than any dark she had ever imagined. Thick, intense, and pulsating, it had a black heart. The hair on the back of her neck rose. How could she possibly enter?

What if a third option lay inside?

"Come closer, my child," said the Dark Lord.

"I ... I can't."

"You're almost here, my child. Come to me. I will comfort you."

"No. Please, I beg of you ..."

"One more step."

Sid. She had to save Sid. She swallowed. Could she save Sid? Should she save Sid, at the expense of others? Cassie closed her eyes and took one step. The darkness swallowed her whole and she shrieked.

"Cassie. Cassie." Her shoulders shook as she heard her name being called.

"Come back to us." It was a man's voice, but not Erebus and not Sanjay's. "Come. Back. To. Me."

"Alessandro?" she called out. "Alessandro, is that you?"

The shaking stopped. His cold arms encircling her, pulling her out of the black ooze into their world, holding her close to his hard, warrior chest. He rocked her as he whispered in her ear. "Fight him, my cherished one. You can do it."

"No," she cried. "I can't. I can't see you."

"Pull the magic from inside you," the vampire said. "Fight him."

"I ... I'm trying," she called back, but what was the use. Black ooze covered her body, penetrating her senses, reaching for her soul. Everything looked so dark. Everything felt so dark.

Suddenly, the vampire let go of her, and she wept. From the bottom of her heart, and the depths of her soul, she wept. It was over. Erebus had her. Had her for eternity. The Evil Lord had won.

Alessandro appeared at her side in the darkness. She could see him now.

"We will fight the darkness, together, my love."

TWENTY-NINE

"Even bad coffee is better than no coffee at all." ~ Davind Lynch

A streak of sunlight hit the floor of Sanjay's dungeon. He examined it carefully. Magic was afoot!

If he could only reach it. Someone had sent him a lifeline and he couldn't damn well reach it. He hung his head back. "Think, you moron," he said to himself. It could be Cassie, but she hadn't developed her skills that far yet. Most likely it was Donovan.

He had found a way through Brackenfeld's protection wards. They had sent him a life jacket. All he had to do was reach for it.

So close, yet so far away. The beam of light was within an arm's reach, but his arms were held in shackles.

"Guard! Guard!" he yelled.

An old man shuffled to his doorway. With the blood-shot, weary eyes of an alcoholic he glared at the warlock. His breath reeked of garlic and onions. "What do you want?" he said. "You know I can't let you out. Not for all the gold in the six realms. You know you cannot threaten me because you are bound by black magic. So, what do you want?"

"Water. I need water," said Sanjay.

"You had water an hour ago."

"I need another glass. Please. I feel as if ..." His voice grew weak. "Your master wants me strong, so he can sell me for a high price."

"Hah. He doesn't care if you're alive or dead. Tell me another story, mage."

"I am a sorcerer, a wealthy and powerful man of magic. I can conjure you your heart's desire. Just give me one glass of water."

The old man frowned. "My heart's desire, you say?"

"Your heart's desire."

A slow smile spread across his round face. "I'd like a wench, a real live and willing wench. Not a hologram, but a real woman."

"A wench it shall be. Blond? Brunette? Red Head?"

"Large breasts. The size of watermelons."

"I can do that."

"Red hair to her waist."

"Got it. Long red hair, big breasts, the size of watermelons."

"And, a plump bum."

"Got it. Red hair, big breasts the size of watermelons, and a plump bum," Sanjay repeated.

"And ..." The guard hesitated.

Good grief. Would this man ever get on with it? He licked his parched lips.

The guard narrowed his eyes. "Willing, you understand, she must be willing."

"Red hair, big breasts, rounded bum and very, very willing." Would he like fries with that?

"Tall. Tall like an Amazon princess, with cocoa-colored skin and full, bee-stung lips."

"Okay," said Sanjay. He ticked off the man's requests on his fingers. "A red headed Amazon princess, with cocoa-colored skin, breasts the size of watermelons, a rounded bum, a willing temperament and sensuous lips."

"You can do that?" The man's beady eyes widened, and he stepped closer to Sanjay, swamping him with foul breath. "Really, you can do that?"

"In measure," said Sanjay. "I can conjure you such a lady for your entertainment, for say twenty minutes."

The man's grin grew and his chest expanded. "That would be something."

"But," said Sanjay.

The man snarled. "What ...?"

"I need my hands, and I need to step outside this cell. Brackenfeld has placed spells on this space that inhibit my magic."

The man pursed his lips.

"A willing redhead," said Sanjay. "Wilder than any you have ever encountered."

"Okay. Okay. Here's the deal. I'll let you come into the guard area. If you create my perfect woman, I will bring you water."

Sanjay weighed his options, as he gave the guard the best smile he could manage with a bruised face.

The guard moved forward and stopped in front of the shaft of light. "What's this?" he said.

"The midday light always shines in here," Sanjay lied. "It's my one solace."

The guard studied it.

"A rounded bum ..." said Sanjay. "Perfect for pinching."

The guard walked around the ray of light and unlocked the shackles tethering Sanjay to the stone wall. "No funny business, warlock."

"None at all. I swear on my name, Sanjay Kahn."

Sanjay followed him into the guard area. As soon as he crossed the threshold of his cell, his body re-energize. His magic had been subdued, but not vanquished. He smiled.

They stood facing one another by the man's desk. "Tell me your name, sir, so that I may tailor the spell to you," said Sanjay.

"Jenoah Wilms," he said.

Sanjay nodded. He raised his hands to waist-level. The magic within him throbbed through his veins. He closed his eyes and felt his power. Pulling magic from within, he conjured a flame between his hands and uttered a spell.

The flame danced onto the floor and grew six feet tall. In a blink of an eye the flame turned into a beautiful woman, who fit the guard's description perfectly.

The guard's eyes popped. He held out his arms to her, and she came to him. He got one good look at her curves before her fangs dropped. She hissed her pleasure.

"No. I didn't ask for a vampire," said the guard.

Sanjay shrugged. "You didn't specify the specie. This is Mabel, a friend of mine from the third realm. She is very willing."

The guard opened his mouth to scream, but the vixen transfixed him with her eyes. Sanjay waved her goodbye, and headed back to his cell. His magic would be dampened as soon as he crossed into it, but he was willing to take that chance.

The ray of light still shone in the center of the space. He reached his hand out, and lost all consciousness as he touched the magic.

THIRTY

"Coffee is a language itself." ~ Jackie Chan

At one time, not so long ago, standing beside him made Cassie feel invincible. But even the mighty Alessandro of Amsterdam would not be enough to fight the Lord of all Darkness. "Alessandro, you shouldn't have come."

"I had to come. You are my woman."

She shook her head. "You are the most stubborn male I have ever met."

"You like that."

The black ooze stopped pulsating and retreated, not completely, but enough so that Cassie could breathe more easily. "Are you doing something?" she asked.

"Standing by you," he said.

"I don't understand."

"I am a creature of the night, my cherished one. I have, let us say, a relationship with the Lord of Darkness. He likes what vampires do, so for the most part he respects us."

"So, he doesn't want you here."

"I suspect Erebus wanted to swallow you up, to devour your witch power. But I am, let us say, indigestible to his system, as I am already a part of him."

Cassie squinted. Too much information. "I never thought of you that way."

"Cassie, my love, when you let me bring you into eternal life you will understand that dancing with the devil is not a big price to pay for eternal pleasure."

"I won't willingly take that step," she said. "You know this."

He growled. "When this feud ends, you may see things differently. My life is not that bad. I have other wives who can ..."

"Wait." What the mother of all witches did he just say? "You have wives?"

"Well, of course. You didn't think a man could live for hundreds of years and not get hitched, did you?"

If only she had listened to her family. Alessandro wasn't the man, she thought he was, at all. She looked around. The blackness had receded and the castle shrunk into the ground. Light permeated the stormy skies. Even the crows had stopped their racket.

"Sid?" she called out. "Sid?"

Her cat's faint meows came from a distance away. She ran through the crumbling castle until she found her sprawled on a large granite bolder. Blood coated her fur.

"Oh, Sid." She pulled the familiar into her arms, and found herself awake in her bed. Alessandro stood by her side.

Pulling magic from every cell in her body she willed it through her fingertips and ran them over Sid. Slowly her familiar healed to her touch.

She turned to Alessandro. "Thank you."

Their eyes locked. "You will always be my favorite," he said. "I promise you that."

Cassie looked closer at the vampire. Blood trickled out of his right ear. "Alessandro, you're bleeding," she said.

"It is nothing. The outer pressure is different in the two realms, and going back and forth gives me a headache." He leaned towards her. "But you are worth it."

Goosebumps rose on her arms. The coolness of his body swept over her, seductive in its own vampiric, supernatural way, but not welcomed. She shivered.

His eyes softened. "Cassie, I love you as I have loved no other woman."

"I know ..." she said.

"We had five good years together." He ran a hand through her hair. "Five unforgettable years."

"I'm with Sanjay."

"Passion. Long nights of passion, that seemed endless," the night stalker continued.

"Sanjay," she said.

"Was a nice distraction," he said. "But let me remind you about us. You smiled and laugh when you were with me. You don't do that anymore."

She winced.

"Cassie, when you are with him all you do is talk about a door, and saving the world. What a waste of time."

"We're fighting Erebus."

"But that's not all of it, and you know it. You are a changed witch. Sanjay is not the man for you. He makes you serious. When was the last time you painted?"

His hands massaged her shoulders. "The warlock is like an appetizer. I am the main course."

Cassie snickered. "Alessandro, we had something wonderful, and I will always remember it fondly."

"Fondly," he grumbled. "That sounds like something you would say about a trip to a flower garden."

His fingers dug deeper into her body, relaxing the tension that rested there. He knew her weak spots so well. Cassie swallowed. "Alessandro, you are right about one thing," she said.

"Yes." He leaned in and whispered in her ear. "I recall you telling me I'm more than right."

"I have changed," Cassie said.

He touched his forehead to hers. "Yes, you have, my cherished one. You are more powerful. But I don't care about your witchiness, or your power. I never did. What I love is your heart, your compassion, your creative soul. Those are the things that make you, you." His soft lips brushed her neck gently, and she could feel his fangs emerging. "That is what I fell in love with five years ago, and what I'm still in love with now. I want you by my side for eternity."

Alessandro had never been so open about his feelings, preferring to demonstrate them physically. Who knew he could talk love so well. A lump caught in her throat. He had meant so much to her. They had been good together. She had laughed and danced. He got her, and her love of art, in a way Sanjay didn't. She looked into his eyes and memories of their time together flowed through her. She sighed.

"I prefer to stay mortal," she said. "It defines me."

"Well, we have many years to debate that, my love. For now, just agree that when this battle with Darkness is over, you will come back to me, to my home, to my bed. Give me one more chance."

She pushed at his rock-hard chest. "I can't. I appreciate you saving my life, but I am not yours. I am with Sanjay."

"Lover, I can offer you so much more than a warlock. I offer you pleasure and happiness for eternity."

A silver mist filled the room. "Take your hands off her," said Sanjay as he materialized beside the bed.

THIRTY-ONE

"I'm just waiting to see if my coffee chooses to use its power for good or evil." Koffee Addict, Facebook

Holy mother-witcher, thought Cassie. Her head swam with images of darkness, her ears ached with the echoes of Erebus's voice, and her heart burned from the scorching heat of fear.

Despite all of that, and despite the nearness of Erebus, these men dared to treat her as property. She groaned, "Get out of my witching space."

She hadn't meant to use magic with her words, but the gravity of all she had gone through spiked her energy, and as her voice grew louder a current of air swirled around them. The lights of The Perfect Brew flickered in response, and the floor trembled. Never had she felt more powerful.

The men turned and stared.

Donovan arrived through a flaming portal on the east side of the room, and Merlina through her own entrance on the west.

"Well, little sister you have grown," said Merlina.

"Shut up," Cassie said. "We have work to do. There's no time for drama." She gave Alessandro a withering look, "Or, ultimatums."

Sanjay's bruised face lit up. "Tell us what you know."

Cassie wanted to run to him, hold him in her arms, tell him how much she had missed him; tell him how much she had feared for his life. But she meant what she said. There was no time for their drama. Their individual lives meant nothing compared to the battle they were up against. Like Rick in *Casablanca* said, "... the problems of three little people don't amount to a hill of beans in this crazy world."

She swallowed and closed her eyes to concentrate. "Erebus came to me in a dream. He's grown more powerful in this realm. If Alessandro had not come to my aid, I would ..." She opened her eyes and looked at the vampire.

The vampire completed her sentence. "... have been changed. But you are not. Let's move on."

"I hate blood-suckers," Sanjay mumbled.

Donovan clapped him on his back. "Not the time, buddy. Not the time."

Sanjay growled.

Donovan continued. "We need everyone on deck. The Brotherhood sent a team of warriors who are helping Henderson and his brigade clean the streets."

"What happened on the streets?" asked Sanjay. "By the way thanks for sending the shaft of magic my way."

"You're welcome. We need you, after all," said Donovan with a smirk.

Sanjay smirked back.

"Erebus," Donovan continued, "sent a pack of demonic wolves through town. Most people got to shelter, but a few did not."

Sanjay winced. "The body count?"

"All the mundanes, with the exception of Gavin, made it to safety. We lost three shifters who died fighting."

"Gavin?" said Sanjay.

"He's in the hospital in stable condition," said Merlina. "Jane is watching over him. He has a deep bite. Right to the bone."

Sanjay nodded and looked at Cassie. "I'm sorry I wasn't here for you."

"We need to act," said Cassie. "I have no idea how to wage war, but if it's war Erebus wants, it's war he gets."

Donovan gave a slight bow to her. "Our warriors are waiting for us. I'll call in the Brotherhood warlocks as well."

"A few vampires should arrive soon," said Alessandro.

Everyone nodded their agreement. Donovan, and Merlina vanished. That left Cassie standing between Alessandro, and Sanjay.

The men glared at each other.

Cassie closed her eyes. Every cell in her body ached. Fighting with Erebus had bruised her to her very soul. Nausea and exhaustion fought to take control of her body, and terror, her mind. Silently she chanted a strengthening spell, and felt her energy returning.

They stared at her. "I'm ready," she said.

Sanjay conjured a flaming silver portal and they stepped through it.

THE WONDERFUL THING about magic is that it can stretch to the occasion, thought Cassie as she noticed the meeting room in The Keep had grown to accommodate their supernatural army. Her breath caught as she scanned the room. The three leaders of the Warriors, Hank Henderson, Pussy Nip and Zatara stood together in one corner.

Nine warlocks from the Brotherhood who stood beside them. On the opposite end of the room, five European vampires leaned against the wall as if this event bored them to the bottom of their black souls. Three of her sisters, Katrina, Crystal and Eleanor, her mother, and her father huddled in conversation next to them. While it was gratifying to see how many supernaturals had come to their aid, the thought of any of them being hurt terrified her. She swallowed, and dug deep, for words to convey her feelings.

Zatara tapped the floor three times, and silence flowed through the room.

Donovan motioned with his arm for everyone to take a seat. "Thank you, good folk, for coming," he said.

"This will be the greatest battle of our time," said Zatara. "It is fitting we fight together. Erebus, the Lord of Darkness, must be pushed out of our realm."

Cassie spoke. "Donovan, do you have a plan?"

In the center of their circle a swirl of dust rose from the stone floor. Higher and higher it grew into a cylindrical shape. Particles swirled around and around until they congealed into the shape of a woman.

Zatara raised his staff ready to defend himself. The warriors raised swords. The witches stretched out their hands. And the vampires coiled for action.

The woman's distinctive face took shape. Great-aunt Ophelia stood before them. She winked at Cassie. "Always make a good entrance, dear," she said.

Cassie's mother spoke first. "Sister, how could this be? Are you the work of the devil?"

"No. I am the work of my own magic, and I have come to warn you."

Sanjay put his weapons away, and the warlocks followed his lead. "Then warn," he said.

"Erebus knows your weaknesses."

"What are you saying?" Zatara's voice demanded.

"He knows you. All of you. Inside and out. He knows everything about you, and you know nothing about him. That is the way of evil. If you are not very careful, you are doomed."

Cassie's chest tightened. She really didn't need to feel any more scared than she already did.

Her mother stepped forward. "Ophelia, are you alive?"

"No," Ophelia responded. "Well, not exactly. I no longer live in your realm, but before I died, I used magic to keep part of me alive in another. I exist, but I have no body. This ..." She waved a hand around her figure. "... is a fancy holograph."

"And you've been watching," said Cassie. That explained why she always felt as if she were being watched.

"Yes, my dear, I have, and you have done well, so far. But now the moment of crisis is upon us."

Cassie's father grumbled "Ophelia, get to the point."

"Mark my words, the Lord of Darkness will attack," She stopped and looked around the room. "He will attack ..." her voice grew weaker. "Where each of you is the most vulnerable."

"Riddles. Witching riddles," mumbled Donovan. "Speak straight, Ophelia."

"I have spent the last nine months watching him watching you. I don't know for sure what he will do, but I can guess his moves."

"Speak, witch." Zatara thumped his staff on the rock floor and raised his hands offering her his magic to keep her in the room.

Ophelia's temporal body blinked in and out of the

realm. She closed her eyes, and in a voice of power said, "I have consulted the oracles. This is his plan."

The air in the room cooled.

"The vampires ..." she nodded at Alessandro, "will be attacked during the day, so they must be well hidden. Cassie must not sleep because he will attack her in her dreams. Shifters will be forced by demonic wolves to shift for battle, and they will be killed during the changing process. Witches and sorcerers will be burned by the mundanes in this town, who will be tricked into thinking they are the evil ones who have brought this madness to their world. And the warlocks ..." Ophelia stopped and looked around. "The warlocks will be left to last." She stared at Sanjay. "They will be killed by their own magic, a spell that reverses the direction of their incantations will bring them down."

"We will not wait for his plan to start," said Sanjay. "We will attack him."

"May the force of goodness be with you," said Ophelia as her image disappeared.

THIRTY-TWO

"To me, the smell of fresh-made coffee is one of the greatest inventions." ~ Hugh Jackman

Cassie watched in awe, as Ophelia's image faded before them. The woman made as impressive an exit, as she did an entrance. "What now?" she said to Sanjay.

He stood. "Ophelia's predictions make sense. Let us address each issue."

Alessandro, never one to sit for long, stood. "The vampires will fight alongside you in any battle, but we expect to be guarded during the daylight."

Donovan spoke from his seat. "We prepared a lower section of the Keep for your use. Protection charms and wards will keep you safe there during the day. I trust you will find our accommodations comfortable."

Pussy Nip in her perfect spandex figure stood. "I'll call a meeting of all the shifters in the region and share Ophelia's concern about our vulnerability. There are things we can do to protect ourselves during transitions. We can double up, and use magic to increase the speed of our shifting."

One of the warlocks stood, a virile rogue of a warrior. "I am Blake and I would gladly shadow you Ms. Nip, and keep you safe."

The other warlocks laughed, until Donovan raised his hand. "That is a good idea, Blake. Each of the warlocks will shadow a prominent shifter." They nodded in response.

The deep voice of Zatara rose. "Good. Good. It sounds like we are already forming a solid defense plan. Now it is time to talk battle strategy."

Donovan rose. "A designated representative from each group should stay for this discussion. With Sanjay's approval, Blake will escort the rest of you to his estate to eat and rest. We will gather together for a final discussion later in the day."

Sanjay nodded. "Of course. You are all most welcome in my home. Just ignore my ghost George. He's harmless."

Alessandro looked down his nose at him. "A ghost? You keep a ghost?"

Sanjay shrugged.

"I don't know about the rest of you, but I could do with a stiff drink, and I know where Sanjay keeps his liquor," said Blake. He moved his arms in an arc pattern and created a large, flaming portal. The guests followed him through.

Cassie nodded at her family to follow the others, but she remained in the Keep. Sanjay put his hands on her shoulders. "We will talk soon, my love. You should go now."

"I thought I would never see you again," she whispered.

Sanjay's marmalade eyes warmed. He leaned in and touched his forehead to hers. "You won't get rid of me that easily."

Alessandro groaned. No doubt he heard it all.

Donovan cleared his throat. "It is time to begin."

Cassie wanted to throw her arms around Sanjay, touch his soft lips, but she pulled away. "I would stay if I thought I'd be useful. But I'm not a warrior. I look forward to seeing you later." Without even thinking about the process, Cassie vanished and reappeared in Sanjay's den. Her magic had taken another giant leap, but she really didn't care about that. Could this day get any weirder?

SANJAY WATCHED as the strategy group took their seats around the war table. The leaders of the Warriors—Henderson, Nip and Zatara—remained. Alessandro, avoided eye-contact with Sanjay, and sat on the opposite him. Merlina, representing the Black family of witches sat next to the vampire. Although it was a formidable group of supernaturals, Sanjay wondered if they would be strong enough and smart enough to beat Erebus, and he knew they shared his concern.

The predator gave Sanjay a side-glass that would kill a mere mortal man, but he chose to ignore it. The leader in him knew he had to act in a mature manner, but he sure as hell didn't want to. What the hex was Alessandro doing in Cassie's dream? Had she slept with him, and the proximity of their bodies allowed him to slide through into her mind? She wouldn't do that. Would she? It didn't make sense. How had the vampire saved her life?

He had so many unanswered questions. But he swallowed his fears and extended his hand to the vampire. "Thank you," he said. "For saving Cassie."

Alessandro looked at his hand and then his face, as if he thought it were a trick. "I didn't do it for you." His fangs dropped and his lips curled as he hissed.

Zatara thumped his staff on the ground. "Enough. Save your pissing contest later."

Donovan's smirked. "Let us begin."

For the next five hours the group discussed battle strategy. They talked flanks, and Trojan horses; magical light shows and dark curses. But not one of their ideas garnered everyone's assent.

"How does one beat the Lord of Darkness?" muttered Sanjay as he rubbed his temple.

"With light," answered Merlina.

A wide smile broke across Donovan's face "That's it."

THIRTY-THREE

"Today my coffee needs a coffee." ∼ Anon, Facebook

At Sanjay's manor, perched on a high cliff overlooking the ocean, the rest of the army prepared for battle. The vampires snoozed on sofas in the basement, while the warlocks raided Sanjay's bar and played his record collection in his study. The Black family of witches gathered around the table in the kitchen, and caught-up on each other's lives. Cassie told them everything she knew about how Ophelia created a haven for magic folk

George, the ghost, burned through all his tricks in the first thirty minutes. He rattled chains, slammed doors, made farting sounds that echoed through the hallways, and danced on the table. All to no avail. The vampires yawned. The warlocks laughed. And the Black family banished him from the kitchen. Realizing no one in this mongrel group of supernaturals was the least bit scared of him, he retreated to the attic to pout.

Flaming messages flew back and forth between the Keep and Sanjay's estate, as the battle plan took shape. At precisely seven o'clock everyone gathered for dinner in Sanjay's grand hall.

A crew of kitchen witches from The Brew prepared a fine feast. Roasted chickens with roasted vegetables from local farms, wine from the mainland, cheese from Amsterdam, and chocolate from Belgium. The blood came from Alessandro's personal supply.

A string quartet of Fae played Vivaldi's Four Seasons as they dined on a meal fit for a conquering tribe.

"More like a last supper," said Sid out loud.

Merlina gave the cat a dirty look. "Can't you scratch fleas somewhere else?"

Sid lifted her chin, but said nothing.

Sanjay raised his wineglass. "The tension in this room is thick enough to give a gargoyle indigestion. We are not all compatible. Nor will we ever be. But we will unite in this fight."

Alessandro laughed, and the vampires followed his lead. Dark chortles all around. The warlocks chuckled in a manly way, and finally the witches snickered.

"To victory," said Sanjay. They all raised their glasses and drank.

Donovan stood and the room stilled. "We attack at midnight. Enjoy your meal. Afterwards we will talk."

The bottom of Cassie's stomach dropped to the floor. Midnight!

THIRTY-FOUR

"Without coffee I literally can't even." ∼ Anon. Facebook

First came the locusts.

Their yard-long antennae twitched in the air, feeding one group mind with information. Real locusts live in Africa and eat carob beans, but these mutant, super-sized beasts stood three-feet tall, and had a six-foot wing span. Their teeth, sharper than a warlock's dagger, shined in the moonlight. The sound of their feet echoed through town as they marched down the main street and slid through the side avenues, devouring any person in their way.

Warnings on Facebook and Twitter spread fast. People hid behind barred doors and prayed. Some tried to phone for help, but cell phone signals were blocked and telephone lines cut. Erebus wanted control.

Four talented sorcerers led by Zatara formed a line as the demonic locusts approached The Brew. Summoning their powers, the wizards unleashed a magical fire that swept through the insect legion in seconds, burning them to the ground. The foul smell of their burnt flesh rose in the air.

The crackling of the fire and the putrid smell pulled the mundanes out of their hiding spots. Cassie's heart bled for them. She couldn't tell them the truth. That would be too scary. But she had to tell them enough to keep them out of harm's way. What should she say?

"Tell them part of the truth," said Sid. "Enough to appease their sense of reality, which is falling apart."

Cassie walked out to the sorcerers who held their place in case a second wave arrived. People gathered around them, shouting questions.

"Who are you?" one woman yelled.

"What were they?" yelled a man.

"Have aliens attacked?" yelled another.

Cassie raised her hand to quell the noise. "I will explain," she said, in as authoritarian voice as she could conjure. The crowd stared at her. Supernaturals in the crowd worked their way to the edges, readying themselves for escape.

"I am a witch," Cassie said.

A murmur rose in the crowd as people turned to their neighbors to say that they had already known that.

"And there are other witches in town," Cassie continued.

More murmurs, as people stepped away from where she stood.

"But do not worry, for I am a good witch."

"Yeah right," yelled a man from the middle of the crowd. "You're trying to kill us."

"I would never do that," Cassie said. "Witches didn't create the demonic wolves or the hybrid-cyber locusts. But, we did ask other supernatuals to help us. These four sorcerers stopped them with magic."

The magi bowed and vanished.

The crowd stared in disbelief.

"The supernaturals in town will do everything in our power to protect you," said Cassie.

"Who is sending these creatures?" asked Mabel, the librarian.

"There is evil in this world and it's trying to overtake our town. From there it will spread throughout the world. We must do all we can to stop it."

More chatter.

"If we stick together, we can win this battle," said Cassie.

The crowd grew silent.

"I ask that you all stay inside, and bar your doors. Do not come out until you get the all-clear signal. No matter what comes to your door, do not open it. Evil has many faces. Evil is devious. You must be on guard."

"I drank some bad whisky," said one of the town drunks.

"I know. Trust me I know. If you had told me a week ago that this would be happening to us today, I would have told you, you were out of your mind. But it is happening. Right here. Right now. We must stand together."

"Or?" said a voice from the back.

"Or, we will die together and the world will be over-run." Cassie's voice trembled with power as she spoke, and they listened.

Mabel, the librarian, walked forward. "Tell us one thing."

"Anything."

"Did the witches bring evil to this town?"

"No, we did not," Cassie said. "We were brought to this town to fight evil."

"Burn the witches. Burn them all. There's no such thing as a good witch." A voice in the back shouted out. Others echoed his voice.

Before Cassie could answer him, the ground beneath her feet shook. A rumbling sound flowed through the town. "Run and hide," she yelled. "Don't come out of your homes, until I tell you to."

THIRTY-FIVE

"Coffee is not a drink. It's a lifestyle." ~ Grab Your Coffee
meme, Facebook

Second, came the snakes. Long snakes, short snakes, and slimy, snakes. Snakes of all dimensions slithered up storm drains and slid through the streets hissing, filling the air with the smell of sewage.

The mundanes, glued their faces to their windows and watched in horror as the reptiles flooded the streets.

The witches formed a circle in the middle of the main street in front of The Brew. Merlina used a wand to draw a flaming pentagram on the pavement. Slowly, they chanted, repeating over and over again, a protection spell, as old as time.

As the reptilian hisses grew louder, so did the witch's incantation. As the snakes neared the circle, Cassie stepped into the center of the pentagram. The rest of the witches, clasped each other's hands forming an indestructible chain.

Cassie drew all her magic. Its power within her had always terrified her, but she could no longer supress it. She let it grow inside her until she lit into a flame. It felt strange to be transformed into fire, but part of her thought it not strange at all. She let her flames flicker high into the sky.

As the first snake darted its tongue at the circle. Cassie raised her flaming arms to the heavens, "I call on all the goodness of the universe to come to our aide." Her words echoed through the town.

Lightning flashed from her finger tips, and a hard rain fell. It turned to acid as it hit the skins of the reptiles and burned through to their flesh. Within minutes all of the snakes were dead.

The flames of magic emanating from Cassie died out. The first thing she saw was Sanjay standing in front of her. He raised his right brow. "Remind me not to make you mad."

If she had any energy left, she would have laughed, but the fight had taken everything from her. "What will Erebus do next?" Cassie asked.

"I hope it won't be a plague. I hate plagues," said Jane, who threw her arms around Cassie. "You were amazing," Jane said.

Merlina conjured a respectable dress for Cassie who stood naked before everyone. The other witches hugged and took refuge in The Brew.

Cassie looked around at the street littered with dead snakes. They were back to waiting, and wondering, and waiting some more. The waiting was the worst part, Cassie thought. Her imagination wandered to strange places. Erebus was the Lord of Darkness, the essence of all evil, the ultimate bad guy. He could command and unleash all the nastiness that exists in the universe. How could they keep fighting him?

"Nah," said Sanjay, reading her mind. "I don't believe he's that powerful."

"Why is that?" said Donovan who appeared, along with Zatara and Alessandro.

"If the Lord of Darkness was truly as omni-powerful as he pretends to be, he would have taken over the world long ago. He keeps trying, but he never succeeds. In the end, love and goodness win."

If she ever wondered why she loved Sanjay, she needed only to remember this moment, thought Cassie.

If only she could take a nap, thought Cassie, feeling her eye lids dropping.

"Do we have any idea when the next attack is coming?" asked Merlina.

"No, but we will know when it starts." said Donovan. "The warlocks and shifters will be on the frontline next."

Zatara tapped his staff on the ground. "The sorcerers have rested long enough. We will take the right flank."

"And the vampires the left," said Alessandro.

THIRTY-SIX

"Live life today like there isno coffee tomorrow." ~ Meik
Wiking, *The Little Book of Hygge*

At the stroke of midnight, as the full moon lit the sky, Erebus attacked. An army of giants marched down the mountain side looking as ugly and invincible as something from Cassie's worst childhood nightmare.

The sound of their feet pounding on the ground grew so loud it was almost deafening. Hundreds of one-eyed beasts marched ten abreast.

The witches, refusing to be sidelined, gathered behind the sorcerers, and with them stood Gavin McGee. The whole staff of kitchen witches from The Perfect Brew linked arms. Stormy, the oldest of all the town witches, stood at the very back, with her chin held high and her aura strong. The familiars stood by the sides of their witches, ready for anything that came their way.

Zatara tapped his staff three times, and twenty wizards spread out to line both sides of the street. They raised their hands to the heavens and called for strength.

Pussy Nip shifted into her full werecat form, and the other shifters followed suit, lining up beside her. Eight werewolves, six panthers, three tigers, and two gargoyles.

Earnest, the dragon, hovered above them shooting flames into the sky.

With folded arms, Alessandro stood in the middle of his cohort of vampires. They displayed an effortless listlessness that felt dangerously eerie. Cassie knew by the tight lines under Alessandro eye's he was anything but relaxed. Creatures of the night never showed fear. They saved their energy for the fight. They were locked and loaded.

Donovan and Sanjay stood in front of thirty warlock warriors buzzing with magic, ready to strike the first blow. Cassie wished she could stand beside Sanjay, but she understood the battle plan. Each supernatural must do their own part, and hers was backup at this point.

As the first ten giants stepped onto the Main street, the wizards released their power. A lightning show, such as Cassie had never seen, lit up the sky. Lightning bolts of all different colors zigzagged through the air decapitating giants as they moved forward. The bodies of the Goliaths continued for a few steps without their heads, and then they dropped to the pavement raising dirt and making a loud thudding sound.

The next ten walked over the first ten, and were felled by more of the wizards' lightning bolts. The crowd cheered, but the battle was far from over. Cassie worried that theatrics would not be enough to stop such a large and powerful army.

Shields magically appeared in the hands of the third group of giants. They raised them to block the wizards's magic. The lightning bolts bounced off the surfaces, leaving the giants unharmed.

Earnest flew above them, and incinerated them with his fiery breath. He felled about fifty before he moved off to recharge his energy.

Closer and closer the evil horde marched towards them.

With supernatural speed the vampires attacked from the side. The giants, caught off guard, fought back. Shields fell. Fangs dropped and so did the giants. They tumbled onto the ground fighting off the creatures of the night. Shrieks of pain filled the air.

The next group of giants marched forward, as if unaware of the fate of their brethren. This time the warlocks attacked. Swords and daggers clashed. Men swore. Magic spells filled the air. The smell of death lingered as the giants fell.

Yet another group of giants pushed forward. Cassie could see no end to Erebus's army. Ogres descended the mountain from as far as she could see.

The shifters leaped onto the next group, tearing at their throats, and biting off limbs. The evil leviathans fought back with swords. The sound of animals crying in pain filled Cassie's heart with terror. The shifters were losing, and they were losing badly.

Cassie scanned the battlefield. All their troops were now in battle. Supernaturals and goliaths filled the center of town, fighting one on one to their deaths. Magic was in the air, but so was evil.

The witches, their final line of defence, grasped each other hands. If they could not hold the evil troops back, then the Lord of Darkness would destroy the town. The mundane would be turned, and the supernaturals devastated.

The giants drew closer. The witches chanted a protec-tion spell, creating a wall of magic, but one beast stepped through the defence and laughed. "You think this can stop us?" he shouted. He strode right through their line, ripping apart their magic wall.

Cassie called on the power within her, and the power of Ophelia. Raising her arms before her, she conjured a ball of fire and threw it towards the beasts. She screamed, "Evil be gone."

Everyone turned towards her. Cassie's cry cut through all the noise and pain of battle, and her magic flames burned through the enemy line from the first giant to the last.

Cassie watched the incineration of the giants as if it were a movie playing on TV, with an odd detachment from the spectacle, as if she were an observer rather than a participant in the center of it all. When the last giant fell, she pulled her magic back inside her heart. The fire she had unleashed vanished. She looked at her hands. What had she done? It felt so surreal.

In her mind's eye she saw the shadow of Erebus withdrawing to the portal door. Sanjay cracked it open with a spell and Cassie slammed it shut behind the evil lord with her own spell. It was over. Erebus, the Evil Lord of Darkness was gone.

THIRTY-SEVEN

"More espresso, less depress." ~ The Singer Cafe,
Betheleham

Sanjay came through the thick layer of smoke that
blanketed the street to stand at Cassie's side. He took her
trembling hands in his. "It's over."

Cassie eyes found his for a minute. Every fibre of her
being knew his words to be true, but her mind struggled for
comprehension.

Why? Why did this have to happen? Why did she have
to be in the center of it? She looked around at the wounded
and the dead. What had she done?

Gently he tucked a tendril of her hair behind her ear.
"I'm sorry you had to go through this."

"I never wanted to fight," she said. "I'm not a warrior.
Not a killer. This is not me." Words gushed out of her. "I
don't like blood. I never in my life wanted to physically hurt
anyone." She swallowed. "It's over, isn't it?"

He nodded. "I believe it is. Erebus will rise again in
some form, but hopefully someone else will fight him." His

arm wound around her waist and he pulled her closer. The sound of his strong, steady, heart beat calmed her nerves. They had survived.

"Yes," he said, hearing her thoughts. "And, you transformed again. You must be one of the most powerful witches alive."

"I don't want to be."

He bowed his head slightly. "That may be. But your magic is profound and you wielded it beautifully."

They stopped talking as the other supernaturals gathered around them. Some came running, others limped, and a few needed to be carried. Cassie scanned their faces, tormented by shock, disbelief, grief, and pain. Victory was not all it was cracked up to be. It would take a long time for them to recover, a long time for her to recover. They would carry scars from this day for the rest of their lives.

This was not what she had wanted for her life. "But it is not for us to decide." Ophelia's voice spoke in her mind. "It was your destiny to fight Erebus. You were given the gifts needed, but it took your determination and your pure heart, to succeed. Do not fear or shun your power. It is a gift you deserve and a gift you will use for good, for the rest of your life."

"But ..."

"I must go now, Cassie," Ophelia said. "I have used up the last of my energy to be with you in this moment. I am proud of you, and honored to be your great-aunt."

A wave of warmth flowed through Cassie's body.

Sanjay raised a brow. "Ophelia was with us through you. She watched it all."

· · ·

TWO AMBULANCES ARRIVED from the local hospital and medics offered their assistance, but the magic folk wanted to be healed by their own. A warlock doctor teleported in from The Brotherhood with a team to help his kind. The witches healed each other. And all the vampires, except for Alessandro vanished to take care of themselves in their own lairs.

It took an hour for the Warriors to clear the wounded from the battle scene. Cassie worked side by side with Sanjay and Alessandro.

Jane went home with Gavin to care for him. He had been there through it all, and was now exhausted. Merlina traveled with the rest of her family back to their hometown in the mountains.

As dawn approached, only the dead giants remained on the battle scene. Mundanes emerged from their homes and offered to take care of them. They said it was the least they could do.

EXHAUSTED CASSIE and Sanjay returned to her apartment. Never had she felt so tired, but beneath the exhaustion she felt a sense of satisfaction. They had beaten back the forces of evil. They had won the day. She looked to her lover.

Mischief sparkled in Sanjay's eyes. They had that warm marmalade color that made her body hum. But so much had happened. They couldn't just jump into bed. Could they?

Cassie cleared her throat. "You haven't told me about what happened to you."

"There hasn't been time," he said. "But, we have the rest of our lives to talk. I will tell you about my abduction. I will tell you whatever you want to know about me and my life as a warlock. There will be no secrets between us."

"I'd like that," she said.

He nuzzled her neck. "But first, you must tell me about Alessandro."

"Hmm. Listen to you, the rogue warlock. You want to share."

Sanjay lifted Cassie's chin. "Yes, my love. I want to share everything. There's no reason for us to hold back on our feelings now. We can finally be one, as we were meant to be."

Cassie pulled back and looked away. "Wait one hex of a minute. We need to take things slower than this."

"Slower?" His voice sounded truly pained.

"So much has happened. You need to think about that. Do you really want to be united with me? Look what I've done. I burned an army." In her mind Cassie shared the image of the dead lying scattered on the ground.

"You were destined to save us, and you did it."

A loving warmth spread through her body." Her breath hitched. His words rang true, and in that moment, she accepted it, all of it. Destiny.

"And you, my love, are destined to be by my side," she said.

"To be your mate," said Sanjay as he leaned in.

THIRTY-EIGHT

"Nothing says coffee like six in the morning." ~ Lorelai
Gilmore, Gilmore Girls

Alessandro appeared beside Cassie. He snorted.

Could his timing be more obtrusive? "You want *him*?"
the vampire said. "Are you sure?"

She looked at the vampire covered in sweat, blood and
what looked like the green entrails of giants. "Yes, I am sure.
My love for Sanjay is stronger than any love I've ever felt. I
am sorry if that hurts you. I am sorry if I have hurt you."

Anger emoted from Sanjay's body in hot waves.
Warlocks are not pleasant to look at when they get mad.
"Stand aside, bloodsucker. Cassie Black is mine. Our bond
is unbreakable. It's time you accepted it."

Alessandro glared at Sanjay. "Hmm. I'll accept it for
now, but that doesn't mean I have to like it."

"Thank you, Alessandro," said Cassie moving her body
to stand between them.

"But there is the tiny matter of our blood bond," said the
vampire.

"Your what?" Sanjay looked at Cassie. "You are bonded to *him!*"

"It's complicated," she said.

"A vampire bond! Did you not think to mention it to me? What the hell, Cassie."

"It can be broken," she said.

Alessandro laughed. "Calm down, warlock."

"I'll kill you," Sanjay raged. "I swear I will kill you. The world won't miss your dead ass." Sanjay pulled his sword from his side and raised it to the sky. "I, Sanjay Kahn, swear," he chanted in Latin, Greek and something else, "I will kill you for this."

Cassie squinted, shook her head, and tried to think of a suitable spell for idiots.

"Not today, my dear warlock." Alessandro folded his arms.

Cassie rolled her eyes and cast her own spell, freezing the men's mouths for a full minute, so she could talk. "We will fix this," she said to Sanjay. "And be together. That is all that matters." She swished her arms and released her spell.

Sanjay sheathed his sword. "How?"

A SMILE BROKE SLOWLY upon Alessandro's face. "I will free Cassie from our bond, because that is what she wants. Let me be clear. I am not doing it for you, warlock."

She mouthed 'Thank You,' to the night stalker.

His ginormous hands encircled her neck. "Do not be alarmed, warlock. I must touch her, to remove my bond."

Sanjay growled. "What the hell?" His marmalade eyes blazed with magic. His hands rose and with them balls of flames ignited.

Cassie shook her head. "It's alright, Sanjay. I trust him. It is something he and I started and must finish. Give us a moment to end it."

Alessandro's brows drew together. "It would be better if we did it during sex."

"Nice try," said Cassie. "We both know that that will never happen again."

"Aah, you can never say never, in this world." The vampire sighed. "I have such wonderful memories."

"Get on with it, deadman," said Sanjay. "I'm right here."

The vampire closed his eyes. "I know, Cassiopeia, there will come a time—I'd like to think many times—when you will remember the two of us together." He leaned down and whispered in her ear. "Call my name at the stroke of midnight, and I will be there for you. No questions asked."

A shiver stole up her spine. Part excitement. Part terror. She pushed at his rock-hard chest to give herself breathing room.

The vampire mumbled a few words, released her neck, and in a flash of a witch's eye, sunk his fangs deep into her neck."

Cassie screamed, and blacked out.

WHEN CASSIE AWOKE MINUTES LATER, she lay in Sanjay's bed, wrapped in his arms. "Welcome back," he said.

"What? What happened?"

"Alessandro removed his bond from your soul. He forgot to tell us it involved a blood ritual."

"I remember the bite."

"He said to tell you, he was sorry it hurt. You passed out

from the pain." Sanjay stroked her hair. "How do you feel now?"

Cassie cuddled into her lover's body, and inhaled his warlock scent—masculine and magical—as seductive as an evening summer breeze. "Free," she said.

"Then, let's celebrate." Sanjay took her face his hands and leaned in for a kiss.

Cassie's whole body lit-up with anticipation. Flames shot from the candles in the room. Rose petals fell from the ceiling. Somewhere, in the distance, music played. Why was she not surprised?

"With this kiss," Sanjay said, "I pledge myself to you, Cassiopeia Black, forever."

"Forever," she said. "I pledge myself to you, Sanjay Kahn. Forever."

"I love you," he said in husky voice.

"Then kiss me, warlock. Kiss me."

And he did. Kiss her. Many times. Until dawn.

THREE WONDERFUL DAYS LATER, as the shimmering pre-dawn light flowed through the open window of Sanjay's bedroom, Cassie woke with a start. Magic, such as she had never experienced, flowed within her. It warmed her body and soul.

Sanjay lay quietly snoring beside her. Though he had gained several scars from the battle, his body remained breath-takingly perfect. So, warlock!

She sighed as she pulled a hand through her messy hair and recalled making love with him for the last three days. Free to immerse themselves in their feelings, their physical entwining had been even more magical than before. And as always, Sanjay's wonderful imagination added spice.

A prickly sensation travelled across her lower belly. She rubbed her hand at the center of it. It couldn't be? Could it?

A faint voice echoed in her ears. "Hi Mom."

Could she know so soon? In her mind's eye she could see a child smiling back at her.

Sanjay always used his magic to prevent a pregnancy, but he must have forgotten to use a spell. She smiled to herself. Nah, he didn't forget. He wouldn't forget something like that. Either he knew exactly what he was doing, or a greater source of magic was at work.

She looked over at his body, exhausted from their marathon of passion. I hope my daughter doesn't snore, she thought.

THIRTY-NINE

"The powers of a man's mind are directly proportioned to the quantity of coffee he drinks." ~ Sir James Mackintosh

George the ghost held Sanjay's front door open, as Cassie tiptoed into the morning light. She needed to return to The Perfect Brew, and after all that had happened, she did not question such a strong, magical feeling of being called.

Back at The Brew, she found not much had changed, and yet everything had changed. How much sense did that make? She encountered, a new-normal as they say.

Oscar and Belle served a long line of customers. The heavenly smell, of coffee mixed with magic, hung in the air.

Supernaturals filled about half of the tables and many of them didn't bother to cloak who their real appearance. What surprised her, and pleased her beyond measure, was that the mundanes appeared not the least bit bothered by seeing the magic folk. They had accepted them.

The Brew welcomed Cassie back with a flash of her lights. As she sat at her favorite table a familiar smelling brew appeared before her. After the first sip, she smiled and waved back at Oscar. It was good to be home, to feel safe, and to feel loved.

Sid jumped on the chair opposite her and purred.

Cassie sipped more of her liquid magic. She didn't have to say anything to Sid. Their contented, silence spoke volumes.

"Not really," said Sid, reading her mind. Her whiskers twitched. "We haven't talked about *everything*."

As she looked at her familiar's black eyes, she noticed that one of them had a twinkle of copper in it. "Your eye?"

"That's nothing," said Sid with a shrug. "I'm talking about Zabrina's murder."

"Oh hex!" said Cassie. "I've been too busy to think about that."

"And yet, you are here," said Sid with narrowed eyes.

Extra-Hot the cop walked through the front door, followed by a chilly winter breeze. It wasn't unusual to see the constable at The Brew, but it rankled her. Cassie shivered.

Why had her magic called her here? Did he have something to do with it? She waved him over.

"Well, hello Cassie," he said in his low rumbling voice.

"Please, join me," she said. "Oscar will bring your drink over. It's on the house."

The cop looked around, as if her offer could be devious, but seeing nothing unusual around him, he took a seat beside her.

Sid's tail swished.

"Have you caught Zabrina's murderer yet?" she asked.

His whole body flinched, and that flinch telegraphed more than she expected. How could that be? Cassie cleared her throat. "I'm sorry," she said. "I shouldn't be so abrupt. How are you?"

He chuckled, and flashed her a handsome smile. "No need to apologize, Cassie. I like direct women. And for the record, I'm doing just fine, thank you." He flashed another toothy smile. "And no, we haven't caught the murderer. We've been too busy helping your Warriors clean up the town, and calming people down."

"Big jobs," Cassie said.

"Yeah, at first, I worried the magic folk would never be accepted by the rest of us, but people surprised me. They're looking beyond the surface and seeing one another's hearts. It's something to watch." He took a sip of his hot coffee. "Look at me. I never would have imagined I'd be talking with a witch."

"I believe my great-aunt Ophelia picked the perfect town for us to come out of the broom closet."

He laughed and took another sip of his brew. "This is so damn perfect," he said. "I have to say, I like living with witches."

Cassie smiled. "So, you haven't had time to think about the murder case."

"Not much." He put his mug down on the table and leaned forward. "Look, I know Gavin shared information with you, but I can't. It doesn't matter if you're a powerful witch. I'm a cop. I could lose my job if I shared stuff with you."

Isn't that a convenient out? "You could tell me what you think of my ideas."

He leaned back and looked at the ceiling for a minute. "Okay. Shoot. What's on your mind?"

"Let me tell you about my investigation. First, I suspected Stardust the singer at The Rusty Anchor, because she was jealous of Zabrina's relationship with her boyfriend, Kylo."

"Stardust had a good motive," he nodded.

"But she has an iron-clad alibi, so I crossed her off my list," said Cassie. "Ditto her boyfriend, Kylo. As painful as I think their love triangle was, it didn't end in murder."

Extra-Hot's face paled at the mention of Kylo's name. Sid jumped onto the floor and wrapped her body around Cassie's feet.

"Yup," he said. "We checked them out. They both have an iron-clad alibi. A bar full of people saw them at the bar that night."

"Fred Thomas," said Cassie, "was my third suspect. He didn't have as solid an alibi, but I just don't think he did it. He loved her. But, he's no killer."

"Anyone can kill," murmured the cop, who picked up his cup with a trembling hand.

Cassie turned on her phone's recording device. "I wondered about Mullins the businessman, next. He pulled his support from Zabrina's studio project, which I thought might have been complicated. I asked him about that, and he explained it wasn't a good business proposition for him. As much as I disliked him, he didn't fit a murderer's profile."

The cop squinted. "Ms. Black you would never make it as a detective. We don't talk about our emotional response to suspects. We look for evidence."

"Some of the best detectives rely on their gut," said Cassie.

He nodded. "That's true, especially on TV."

Cassie smiled. "And my gut says you did it."

Extra-hot dropped his cup and stood. Coffee splashed over the top of the table. "What?"

The Yuskick brothers sitting at a table by the door turned to look at them. Oscar at the bar looked her way, as well. Cassie sensed them summoning their magic to help her.

Feeling emboldened, Cassie spoke. "Zabrina was a beautiful woman, inside and out. Many of us loved her. You shouldn't be ashamed of your feelings, constable."

The words hit him like a sucker-punch. "How dare you suggest I ..."

"Loved her?" Cassie finished his sentence.

"Well, I spent time with her. I won't deny that."

"But she wasn't willing to be exclusive, was she? Zabrina was a free spirit. She started seeing Kylo."

"How did you know?"

"The look on your face. Your pulse. Your scent of deception."

He put a hand to his jaw. "Okay, you got me there. I cared for Zabrina, and I didn't like her being with other men. But that doesn't make me a murderer."

"Charles, You have a motive as old as time. Jealousy. You wouldn't be the first man to kill a woman he loved." She leaned back and took him in with all her senses. Yup, he was guilty. "It won't be hard to find out where you were that night."

Sweat beaded on his forehead. "After work I had a few beers with Gavin, then I went home to watch wrestling."

"You know I know everyone in town, and I hear all the gossip. I can tell you how many eggs Mary Louise's chickens hatched this morning, what weights our high school's star quarterback lifts, how many times Oscar has been asked out today, and even what color underwear the librarian is wearing. My coffee house is a treasure trove of data. And don't forget I am a formidable witch, with sisters who are clairvoyant. Don't try to fool me."

His jaw clenched. His cheeks reddened. She had him.

All she had to do was find evidence. Reel him in like the scumbag he was.

"Or get him to admit it," mumbled Sid in her head.

"Just tell me what really happened," Cassie said. "Get it off your chest. You'll feel better. Trust me, you don't want to lie to a witch."

"I loved her."

Cassie nodded.

The cop sighed. "I didn't mean to ..."

Cassie nodded again.

He looked away. "Zabrina was so beautiful, and loving. I had never been with a woman who made me feel so special. I thought we had something really special, you know, just the two of us. And then I heard Kylo laughing with the guys at the bar, telling them about the dragon tattoo she had on her inner thigh. And I knew. I knew I wasn't her only man."

"So why didn't you kill Kylo?"

"Oh, I wanted to, but I didn't. I'm not a murderer. I went straight to Zabrina's apartment to confront her. The least she could have done was been honest with me."

"And she told you the truth."

"She told me, she was in love with life, and didn't think she could ever love just me. I remember her exact words, 'I could never love a cop.'" He hung his head low. "I snapped, grabbed the street knife I keep strapped to my ankle for emergency and plunged it into her. I didn't think. I just acted."

Cassie thought she should hate him. She should want to kill him. At the very least she should want to yell at him. But all she felt was pity for him, and sadness for Zabrina. He would carry the guilt of killing the woman he loved for the rest of his life. Zabrina had died for her callous treatment of a lover. Life sometimes didn't make sense.

When she didn't say anything, he looked up at her. "I'm sorry," he said.

"I know," she said. "The question is, what are you going to do about it now?"

EPILOGUE

"I think the key to the start of any good relationship is to remember how the other person likes their coffee."
~ J. Lynn, *Waiting for You*

Three months later, Cassie sat at her kitchen table wondering if morning sickness ever ended. She could keep nothing in her stomach. Absolutely nothing. Not even crackers. As soon as she swallowed food acid rose in her throat.

Their witch doctor had no sympathy. She simply hemmed and hawed and declared that the baby must be truly powerful.

How on earth had her mother given birth six times? Cassie held her hand over her baby bump and sighed as her child reached back to her through her mind. The warmth of their bond flooded her senses. The thought of holding her baby in her arms, more than made up for her stomach problems.

Never had she been so happy as she was now. They say people only get everything they ever wanted at the end of a romance book. Her life was not as perfect as all that, but still, she figured she had everything, right here, in this moment.

FIRST OF ALL, she had Sanjay. Their love, which she had thought was as complete as it could possibly be, continued to grow. She had moved into his crazy castle on the cliff, and picked out colors to decorate the nursery. George the ghost had fallen in love with the idea of having a baby in his house, and they had become an unusual but happy witch, warlock and ghost family. They planned to have a celebration of their union and the arrival of the baby the following spring when the roses from the old garden were in full bloom. She wanted wear the wedding dress of her dreams. Jane and Merlina spent a lot of time helping her plan the event.

Waking up in her bed this morning without Sanjay had sucked, but it couldn't be helped. He was an important member of The Brotherhood council and had to attend meetings and the Goddess only knew what else. They had just completed the trial and banishment of Brakenfeld. Never again would he hurt anyone.

Having Sanjay busy with warlock business gave her time to work on her new project, The Mystic Art Gallery & Studio. MAGS for short. Cassie with the help of other artists in town were bringing Zabrina's dream to life. Best of all, Cassie was painting again.

That was her favorite story. A week after the final battle, Sanjay told her he had a surprise. He covered her eyes with a scarf and walked her downstairs. She thought maybe he had brought her a bouquet of flowers, but when he undid her mask, she stood in awe. The former ballroom was no longer filled with dust and memories. Sunlight flooded the space through windows. The wood floor shone with fresh wax. The wainscoting gleamed. The antique crystal chandelier gleamed in the sunlight reflecting rainbows throughout the room. It was like walking into an enchanted fairy land. But the best thing of all, was what lay in the middle.

"What have you done?" she asked.

He took her hand. "That's the best part," he said.

In the middle of the room sat a painting easel with an empty canvas on it. A full array of oil paints lay on a table next to it, along with brushes, and an assortment of painting tools. Cassie fought to breathe. "I ... I didn't think you knew," she said.

"Knew what," said Sanjay who stood behind her.

"How much painting means to me."

"Oh, I knew," he said. He grabbed her by the waist and turned her around for a kiss. "I always knew."

It was a moment she would never ever forget.

SO, thought Cassie, I'm marrying my perfect man, having his child, and I'm painting again. Life doesn't get better than that.

BUT THERE WAS MORE. There was definitely more.

The sleepy town of Mystic Keep had not only survived the great battle, it had grown in ways she had never imagined. The hashtag-burn-the-witches was replaced by hashtag-diversity-rocks! How cool is that?

The town embraced witches, warlocks, shape shifters, sorcerers ... basically anything that came there way with good intentions. Ophelia's dream of creating a haven for supernaturals had grown beyond her greatest dreams.

Life in town surged with energy, creativity and love. The Mystic Warrior group grew larger and stronger. The Perfect Brew was always busy. And ...

"SHEESH," grumbled Sid, who lay on the windowsill, bathing in sunlight. "Your hormones are making you crazy again."

"They are not," said Cassie.

"Are too. Not everything in life is perfect. It never is. And the moment you begin to think it is, you know what will happen."

Cassie picked her cat up and stroked her fur. "Yeah, yeah, it's bad luck."

"And?" said Sid wiggling her whiskers.

"Okay, I'll admit it, everything in my world is not perfect."

"Good. Now let me sleep again."

Cassie scratched Sid under her ears and the familiar purred.

"AND, GAVIN TURNED INTO A WEREWOLF," she said. "He's not happy about that, and he keeps fighting with Jane, who has fallen broom over boots in love with him, though she won't admit it."

"And?" said Sid between purrs.

"And, Alessandro left town in a really foul mood. But he's sure to find a new lover and leave Sanjay alone." Or so she hoped.

"And?" said Sid.

"The Yuskick brothers are fighting again."

"Yeah, well, the world is still turning."

She giggled. "True."

"And?" prompted Sid.

"I'm out of bad things. The world is full of good things, and that's what I want to focus on. I could worry about how I'm going to manage my annoying sisters, or how powerful my baby witch will be; but I'm not going to. Things will work out. I know they will. They always do."

Sid lifted her head. "Especially when you choose love."

Sanjay appeared through a silver portal. "Did you call me?" He laughed at his own vanity and swept Cassie into his arms. They kissed.

A FEW MILES AWAY, Sid, Vixen, Peregrine and Zoey stood together on the old wooden bench at the Lookout, watching the sun rising over the mountains.

Sid's whiskers twitched. "Cassie may think the story's over, but it's not," she said. "It's only beginning."

"You want more," said Peregrine.

Sid narrowed her eyes. "Cassie didn't mention us."

Vixen lifted her nose in the air. "You mean you."

"Well, yes. Me, for starters. You might want to know, the demon blood I've lived with for years is out of my system. The doc figures it happened when Cassie cleansed the enemy with fire."

Peregrine chuckled. "No more dirty jokes?"

Sid's whiskers twitched. "I'll keep telling dirty jokes because I like them, but I've stopped craving people's jewelry."

Vixen sighed loudly. "I'd miss your jokes if you stopped them."

Sid's tail flicked.

The falcon clicked his beak. "Truth be told, I'd miss them too, Lady Obsidian."

Sid meowed. "Did the battle change you, Peregrine?" she asked.

"I think it changed us all," he said. "But, I don't like talking about myself. How are you doing Zoey?"

Ophelia's familiar stretched her long, sleek body. "Just fine, darling," she said in a sultry voice. "But I don't understand what happened. I woke up when Cassie screamed, that's all I know."

The bird shuffled his feet. "Okay Sid, let's hear your version of this tale."

Vixen rolled her eyes. "Please, don't encourage her."

The raptor chuckled. "Wait, let me guess. A witch with a talented familiar met a warlock with a handsome and charming bird..."

NOTE FROM JO-ANN

I started this book at my home in the Pacific Northwest before the Covid-19 pandemic hit, and finished it after the first wave. Did the plague affect my writing? Yes. For weeks I couldn't scribble a word.

As I write this note, I'm not sure what will happen next in our fight against the virus, or our struggle for justice.

But I know one thing. We all need stories. I offer you my latest, the third segment in The Perfect Brew trilogy, and I hope you enjoyed it.

I wish you well in these troubling times. Stay safe.

Thank you for reading my book.

Warmest Regards,

Jo-Ann

P.S. To sign-up for my newsletter, find my social media links, and/or learn more about me, go to my website, https://www.jo-anncarson.com.

P.P.S. I'd love it, really love it, if you left me a review on Amazon or wherever you found my book. Sharing is caring, as they say, and reviews sell books.

ACKNOWLEDGMENTS

First of all I'd like to thank by friends and family, whose support and love make all things possible.

I'd also like to thank my professional team:

My beta-readers helped me plug the holes in my stories. Their feedback helps me imeasurably.

Nicole Laverdure,
Barb Cassata,
Darcy Speed, and
Marianne Kay.

My proofreader helped me polish my work:

Tammy Payne

And last, but far from least, my cover designers at:

Deranged Doctor Design

All these people helped me create and polish my story, but the errors, trust me, are all my own.

Trouble brews when a psychic enchantress shares her magic.

When the sorceress Jane Black offers spells, potions, and tarot card readings to the regular folk in her small town, she finds herself in a cauldron of hot water. Despite her good intentions, spells spiral out of control, potions backfire, and people turn against her. As Jane's problems multiply, a drool-worthy dragon enforcer, arrives on her doorstep and gives her an ultimatum. While the universe stacks impossible odds against her, a hot dragon breathes down her neck, and Vixen, her snarky familiar, harangues her every move, Jane refuses to give up. She's determined to make things better for everyone, or die trying. Is Jane's magic strong enough to heal the town's problems? Will her full-service sorcery store, survive? And what exactly will Leos the dragon set on fire? Dial Witch is the first book in the Dial Witch trilogy, set in the Mystic Keep world. It chronologically follows The Perfect Brew trilogy, but can easily be read as a standalone story.

Buy Links

Excerpt - Chapter One

"By the pricking of my thumbs, something wicked this way comes." Shakespeare, Macbeth

"It's a stupid idea," said Vixen.

"They have places for wayward familiars," said Jane Black, as she glared at her orange tabby who sat on her desk facing her.

Vix's whiskers twitched. "I repeat, stupid."

"They don't have sardines in the cold, dark and lonely place I'm thinking about."

The cat raised her nose and looked away. "You can't manage without me."

As Jane considered that thought, she noticed someone standing outside her front window. "See Vix, the masses are gathering."

The cat swiveled her neck. "It looks like one person to me."

The stranger, a middle-aged woman with short brown hair and round tortious-shell glasses, stared up at the sign hanging over the shop's door. *Dial Witch*. Straightening her back, she moved closer and peered into the front window. Jane had spent hours setting up the display, arranging bundled herbs tied with ribbon, potion bottles, and sets of tarot cards to capture the attention of people passing by. The woman tilted her head as she studied the items. Jane held her breath and inched closer to the glass with Vixen at her heels. As the stranger's eyes caught Jane's, her body stilled, and all the color in her face drained. Stepping back, she crossed herself and mumbled, "It's the end of times. The end of times."

It was, in fact, a sunny Monday morning in July, and the witch Jane Black stood with her cat in her new sorcery store waiting for business.

As the woman fled, Jane threw up her hands. "I just want to help," she said. "Why can't people understand a woman wanting to use her power?"

"Like I said. It's a dumb idea," murmured the cat.

"No, it's not," said Jane.

"Regulars don't want help from a witch. They've all read the Grimm tales."

Jane smirked. "Watch it. I'll cross anchovies off the shopping list."

Vix hissed and strode over to her favorite cushion sitting in front of the fireplace. As she settled in, she turned her body, so her bum faced her witch.

"I don't get it, Vix. Why don't regulars at least check us out?" She looked around her witch store. Everything she could possibly need was there. Shelves of books on arcane knowledge lined one wall. Her trusty cauldron, crystal ball, and candelabra sat on a work table in front of a gigantic stained-glass window on the opposite wall. Herbs and potions from every realm filled a storage unit in one corner, and a glass display case filled with decks of tarot cards sat in another. The smell of secrets and magic tinged the air.

Vix shrugged.

"And why the hex isn't anyone calling? I put ads everywhere." Jane pulled out her cell phone and punched the store's phone number.

"Dial Witch, the one-stop shop for sorcery in Mystic Keep," said the recording. She grunted. Her voice sounded stiff and efficient. Maybe that put people off.

Jane started a new recording. "Dial Witch, the town's one and only full-witch-service." That sounded kinky. Jane bit her lip. How could she compress who she was and what she wanted to do into a single slogan?

Vixen, who heard all of Jane's thoughts as if they were her own, turned to face her. "A sound bite."

"Exactly. I need to reduce myself into a friggen sound-bite."

Vix sighed. "Tell me what you have to offer."

"I'm the sixth sister of the sixth sister in a powerful witch family. Should I say that? It's rather confusing." Jane exhaled noisily. "I'm a talented psychic, adept in all sorts of magical practices." She pushed her long, wayward hair behind her shoulders. "People should want my help."

"For a smart witch, you're really dumb sometimes."

"I've done everything I can to make this business work."

Vix pawed the air. "Listen. Regulars grow up believing witches are dangerous."

"We are. What's your point?"

"They think sharing anything about themselves with a witch is the first step to selling their souls to the devil."

Jane shook her head. "That's simply not true."

"And, need I remind you that the regulars aren't your worst problem." Vix swished her tail.

Leaning back as far as Jane could in her fancy new office chair, she put her feet on the top of the desk and admired her pedicure. She wore flip-flops as usual. Who knew going into business would be so hard?

"You don't have to sell your services or run a store. You have nothing—I repeat nothing—to prove."

Jane frowned. "It's not about that. Deep in my heart, I know this is what I'm meant to do."

Vix rolled her eyes. "Keep telling yourself that."

"I figured it would be a success from day one. It makes perfect sense. Everyone has problems. I can help."

Vix blinked. "Okay, let me say this slowly. They don't want your help."

"But I saw it in a vision."

"Forget the vision. The store is a bad idea."

Jane winced. "I know what you're thinking."

"At least one of us is capable."

"Sometimes, my desires get in the way and muddle up my perceptions of the future. I admit that. Not all my visions turn into reality. But this one is different, Vix. I swear. I feel it in my bones."

"First your heart, now your bones. Are you sure you don't have indigestion?"

"Stop it, Vix. The town of Mystic Keep needs healing."

Vixen's eyelids dropped to half-mast.

"I can integrate regulars with supernatural beings, Vix. Right here, right now, in this full-service sorcery. I can do this."

"First, you're a witch. Now you're a healer." The familiar tilted her head.

"Don't you see? Regulars will learn to accept magic as the wonderful thing it is, and the supes won't have to hide their talents."

"It's a noble wish." Vix checked her claw manicure.

Jane shrugged. "What can go wrong?"

"Let me count the ways." Vixen stood, did a 360, and settled back into her cushion.

The front door banged open, and a tall, slender woman strutted into the middle of the store. Bleached and brittle, blonde hair fell over her narrow shoulders. Wearing a tight fire-engine-red dress that hid nothing, she looked like a wannabe runway model, aging badly. Anger blazed in her blue eyes.

Jane stood. "Can I help you?"

The woman strode awkwardly into the room on spike heels and came to a teetering stop in front of Jane's desk. "My name is Elly Briggins, and I have a problem."

Jane inhaled deeply. The client exuded no magical energy. "I'm Jane Black, psychic and magic practitioner. Please, have a seat and tell me more." She motioned to the client's chair.

The woman held her head high as she sat. "It's my husband, Butch."

"Is he not well?"

The woman's eyes narrowed. "I want him out of my life."

"Excuse me?"

"I said." Elly Briggins spoke slowly as if she were talking to a child. "I want him gone!"

"Are you asking me to do what I think you are asking me to do?" Jane sat down.

"Kill him," the woman said. "Take him out. Zap him with the Devil's lightning or something. Just get rid of him."

Jane straightened the yellow pad of legal-sized paper in front of her. "Have you considered couple counseling?"

"Dead, I said. I want Butch dead."

Jane picked up her pencil and drummed the desk. "Why?"

Anger flashed in the woman's eyes. "I want my freedom."

Jane leaned forward. "Did Butch do something?"

Elly exhaled noisily. "I want you to kill my husband. Can I be any clearer?" Her spit flew into space between them. "I'll pay you to do it. I have savings."

Jane looked up at the ceiling for a minute, hoping for inspiration, but all she saw was a water stain.

Her visitor looked around the room as if answers hid in corners.

"Elly, I'm here for you."

An evil smile laced with hope spread across Elly Briggins's thin white face.

"But," continued Jane. "I'm not an assassin."

Elly's shoulders stiffened.

"Tell me more about Butch. Maybe I can fix him."

The woman pursed her lips. "Okay," she said slowly. "Everything about him drives me crazy. He comes home late for supper. He's lazy. His socks smell. He never listens to me. And, he watches hockey every Saturday night."

"How's the sex?"

Elly squirmed as if she sat on a platter of worms. "What business is that of yours?"

"We all need intimacy, Elly. So tell me, is he any good in the sack?"

The woman blinked.

"You know what I'm talking about. Does Butch take you to the moon and back?"

"My husband?"

Jane narrowed her eyes. Why did regulars have trouble talking about something as natural as coupling?

Elly shook her head. "Look, Ms. Black, I don't see why my sex life matters."

"Killing someone is serious business."

"You're a witch. Just do it."

Jane winced. "How about I fix Butch instead. Wouldn't that be better?"

"Fix him?"

"I'll design a potion for him. All you need to do is slip it into his favorite drink, and I promise you, he will be a changed man."

"Changed?" Elly squinted.

"Yes, definitely. He'll be Butch point 2, and trust me, you won't notice the smell of his feet."

"You can do that?"

"Yes. I'm good at fixing men. I know what I'm doing."

Vix chuckled, and Jane gave her a withering look.

Elly's brows met in the middle. "All I need to do is slip him your potion?"

Jane looked up at the water stain. It wouldn't be wise to make her magic look too easy. "There is one thing I need you to do." She lied.

"Name it."

"Make a list of all the things you want me to fix, and bring it to me. Then, I'll add a silent spell to the potion to address those items."

"When will this magic be ready?"

"Come for it tomorrow." Jane stood and offered a fist bump. "Shall we say nine o'clock? The cost will be one-hundred dollars."

Elly's lips mushed together. "It's that simple?"

"Yes. I am a good witch and a competent one. I'll fix the Big Guy." Jane took her fist back.

Elly blinked. "You ... you ... know my pet name for him. No one knows I call him 'Big Guy' when we're alone.'"

"I'm psychic. Remember. Psychic. I can read your mind." And your heart, but Jane didn't say that. "Tomorrow, Elly. I will see you tomorrow. My potion will end all your troubles."

As the front door closed behind Elly Briggins, Jane did a victory jig around the room. Her cell phone dinged with a text message. "Family dinner, TONIGHT!" It was from her sister Cassie.

"I love family get-togethers," said Vix with a sigh.

"That makes one of us." Jane shrugged. It didn't matter. Nothing her family could say about her shop could dampen her spirits tonight. She had her first customer. Things were going her way.

Nothing could go wrong now.

Vix rolled her eyes.

Buy Links

THE PERFECT BREW TRILOGY

All buy links can be found on my website: https://www.Jo-AnnCarson.com

The Perfect Brew
A potion for mystery & magic

When evil rises one clumsy witch must save the world. Cassie Black inherits a sentient coffee-house, complete with an inter-dimensional portal and a side of ancient curse from her great-aunt Ophelia. When Cassie attends the funeral, she discovers the Pacific Northwest town is a haven for supernatural beings. Ophelia's death is suspicious and her lawyer is poisoned.

Up to her neck in mysteries, and weighed down with a mysterious curse, Cassie hunts for the murderer. There are many unusual suspects, a tall, dark and annoying detective keeps getting in her way, and a seductive warlock offers his assistance.

Will Cassie catch the villain before he kills again? Can she protect the portal and still free herself from the curse?

Will Sid, her snarky cat familiar, convince her to play dirty with the boys?

This is the first novella in The Perfect Brew, paranormal, cozy series, which can be read as a stand-alone. If you like stories with strong characters, cozy-styled mystery and humor, you'll love this one. There's no sex or violence on the page, but be prepared for some serious romance, mystery, and magic.

Buy *The Perfect Brew* today to start your own magical adventure in the town of Mystic Keep.

***

A Double Shot of Magic

~ *a recipe for love* ~.
The Perfect Brew Trilogy, book 2
By Jo-Ann Carson

When evil rises, one witch must save the world. Darkness seeps into the small Pacific Northwest town of Mystic Keep, a haven for supernaturals and unsuspecting humans, the kind of place where everyone has a secret. Cassie Black, the owner of The Perfect Brew, a café that serves coffee laced with magic, and protector of the inter-dimensional portal beneath it, fights the darkness with the help of her unusual posse of men, and kid sister, Jane.

Larry, a popular homeless man with a mysterious past, is shot in an alley. Clenched tightly in his hand is a note, "BEWARE BLACK WITCH." The words, written in blood, could mean many things, and none of them are good. As Cassie unravels the mystery of his death, someone tries to murder her.

The very human detective, Gavin McGregor, suspects Cassie is the cause of all the unusual happenings in town and shadows her every move. Her former boyfriend, Alessandro, the vampire, wants her back in his life, alive or dead, and makes his intentions clear. Sanjay Kahn, a wickedly handsome, rogue warlock, vies for her attention and her heart.

A murder to solve, a supernatural curse to wrestle with, and a full dance card ... what more could a good witch want?

A Double Shot of Dead is the second book in the critically acclaimed Perfect Brew trilogy. It can be read as a stand-alone or as part of the series. If you like magical cozies with strong characters, romance, and humor, you'll love this novel.

Buy *A Double Shot of Dead* today and enjoy a fun, heart-warming story filled with intrigue and sweet romance.

A Triple Shot of Trouble

~ Trouble comes in threes

Can an enchantress stop evil from taking over the world? In the third book in the Perfect Brew trilogy, Cassie Black, a powerful witch with a serious caffeine addiction, faces Erebus, The Lord of Darkness who has no weaknesses because he's a pure badass. With the help of a sexy warlock, a vampire who doesn't understand the word "no," and a very-human detective, she searches for a way to banish the Master of Evil forever.

It's been months since the dark lord raised his head, but when an artist in town is murdered, Cassie knows the beast is back. Using all her resources, she searches for her friend's murderer knowing they will lead to the source of all evil.

Will the body count rise before Cassie catches the killer? Will she vanquish Erebus once and for all? It's a good thing her coffee's spiked with magic, because she has a lot on her plate.

A Triple Shot of Trouble is the third and final book in the critically acclaimed Perfect Brew trilogy. It can be read as a stand-alone or as part of the series. If you like magical cozies with strong characters, romance, and humor, you'll love this novel. It has a happy ending.

Buy *A Triple Shot of Trouble,* today and enjoy a fun, heart-warming story filled with intrigue, sweet romance and a touch of magic.

ALSO BY JO-ANN CARSON

Links for all my books can be found on my website: https://www.jo-anncarson.com

Dial Witch Trilogy (2021)

Dial Witch

Dial Sorcery

Dial Magic

The Perfect Brew Paranormal Cozy Mystery Trilogy (2019-2020)

The Perfect Brew

A Double Shot of Magic

A Triple Shot of Trouble

Mystic Cove Universe (2019 -)

A Blind Date for Christmas

Three Reasons Not to Kiss a Warlock

Murder for Christmas (a gothic suspense) (2018)

A Ghost & Abby Series (paranormal mystery) (2017, 2018)

Midnight Magic

I Messed Up Christmas

Death by Seance

Death by Tarot Card

The Gambling Ghosts Series (2016, 2017)
(sweet fantasy, adventure and romance)

A Highland Ghost for Christmas, Novella #1

A Valentine's Ghost for Valentine's Day, Novella # 2

Confessions of a Pirate Ghost, Novella #3

The Biker Ghost Meets His Match, Novella #4

The Vancouver Blues Series

Steamy Romantic Suspense:

Black Cat Blues

Ain't Misbehavin'

Mata Hari Series

Steamy Romantic Suspense:

Covert Danger

Ancient Danger

Lovin' Danger

ABOUT THE AUTHOR

Jo-Ann Carson
A little bit of magic …

Jo-Ann Carson is an award-winning author who loves the magic of storytelling. She creates unique characters, and places them in fast-paced plots, to tell stories about love, friendship, and family.

In her latest trilogy, Dial Witch, the enchantress Jane Black offers spells, potions and tarot card readings to the regular folk in her small town and finds herself in a cauldron of hot water. The cast of characters includes a drool-worthy dragon who wants to light her fire, a blackmailing vampire with his own agenda, two over-protective warlock brothers, and a snarky familiar. Not to mention her meddling sisters, and the fact that none of these characters want her to run a magic and sorcery store.

To date, Jo-Ann Carson has published 24 titles. Her last three series are The Gambling Ghosts, Ghost & Abby Mysteries, and The Perfect Brew. All her books with their buy links can be found on her website.

A firm believer in the magic of our everyday lives, Jo-Ann loves watching sunrises, walking beaches near her home in the Pacific Northwest and reading by a crackling wood fire.

Website: https://www.Jo-AnnCarson.com

Bookbub: https://www.bookbub.com/profile/jo-ann-carson

Goodreads: https://www.goodreads.com/author/show/13499849.Jo_Ann_Carson

Facebook: https://www.facebook.com/JoAnnCarsonAuthor

Twitter: https://twitter.com/Jo_AnnCarson

Pinterest: https://www.pinterest.ca/authorjoanncarson/

www.ingramcontent.com/pod-product-compliance
Lightning Source LLC
Chambersburg PA
CBHW030143180626
46812CB00002B/823